Brass Chains

Donna Kelly

Annie's®
AnniesFiction.com

Library of Congress-in-Publication Data
Brass Chains / by Donna Kelly
p. cm.
I. Title
            2014954972

AnniesFiction.com
800-282-6643
Annie's Mysteries Unraveled™
Series Creators: Janice Tate and Ken Tate
Series Editors: Shari Lohner, Janice Tate, and Ken Tate
Cover Illustrator: Kelley McMorris

10 11 12 13 14 | Printed in China | 9 8 7 6 5 4 3 2 1

One

Kate Stevens brushed a lock of brown hair from her brow as she pushed open the door to the Once Upon a Yarn needlework shop and sighed with contentment. The trio of bells attached to the door jangled as Kate entered and held the door for her friend Vivi Lawrence. Kate never knew what creative magic would transpire under the twinkle lights and among the cubbies brimming with colorful yarn. She loved this place.

They were just passing the small white coffee table where hot beverages were offered in dainty china cups when they heard voices in conversation filtering from the center of the shop.

"Hello. Paige?" Kate led Vivi toward the voices. Vivi followed with a "Yoo-hoo!"

"We're back here by your two formal dresses." Paige Bryant, the shop's owner, waved to Kate and Vivi. She was standing with a striking blond woman in a navy power suit and stilettos.

"This is Kate, the needlework genius behind these gorgeous gowns," Paige said. "She's one of the best in the area. And this is our friend Vivi Lawrence." Paige placed her hand on Kate's bare forearm. "Meet Jamielyn Martinez. She's a wedding planner looking for a designer to create a one-of-a-kind crochet wedding gown."

Dressed to accommodate the summer heat, Kate felt a bit too casual in her white cotton sundress and sandals, but she squared her shoulders and shook hands with Jamielyn. "What season will the wedding be held?"

In a thick Texan accent, the wedding planner clicked off the main details of the event. It would be a garden wedding in autumn. The ceremony and reception would be at the same place. The bride and her mother were still haggling over other details. Kate could tell that the woman was somewhat irritated by the situation.

"The bride is determined to have an October wedding and equally adamant about having a custom-designed and fitted gown," she said. "We're already into mid-August. Is this doable?"

Kate considered for a moment. "If the design isn't terribly complicated and other projects allow, a gown can be crocheted in plenty of time for a late-October wedding."

"Your gowns are exquisite," Jamielyn said, lightly running her fingers over the crystal beading on a pale green, silk-lined, strapless, floor-length dress. "Do you have a card?"

Kate dug through her purse and pulled out the leather-and-silver card case her daughter, Vanessa, had given her to kick off their new lives in Texas just a year earlier. She pulled out a card and handed it to her. "Please feel free to call me if you have any questions about crochet wedding dresses in general or my designs. My website is listed on here, as well as my contact information."

The woman nodded and placed the card in a side pocket of her sizable briefcase purse. "Thank you. We'll keep you in mind."

Paige walked Jamielyn to the shop door while Vivi beamed at Kate. "What fantastic timing we had. You were brilliant." She gave Kate an exaggerated celebratory slap on the back. "She certainly acted like someone important."

"Maybe so." Kate didn't like to count her tomatoes until they were ripe. *You never know when a squirrel will get to it first.*

But even Kate had to admit her career was going well since

she'd moved from a quiet seaside town in Maine to Sage Hills, a small village just outside Fort Worth, Texas. She'd gone from selling a few crochet pieces at A Stitch in Time, a needlecraft store in Stony Point, to writing a series of crochet design books, blogging, and juggling her career's social-media sites. Paige seemed to sell Kate's fashion pieces as fast as Kate could make them.

"She was impressed with your work, I could tell. I'll bet you hear from her." Paige brushed a bit of dust off a wrought-iron dress form. "As you can see, I sold the yellow two-piece casual dress. Do you have anything to replace it?"

"Not at the moment. I've been preoccupied with writing my next book and updating my website and trying to get ahead on my column for *Hook and Needle Arts* magazine. But I'll start something new soon."

Paige nodded. "It's been a busy summer. How are Vanessa's classes going at my alma mater? She should be finishing up the summer session soon."

Kate smiled at the mention of her daughter's name. Vanessa hadn't missed a beat when they moved from Maine to Texas. She quickly found a circle of friends and was doing well academically. Her name had been on the dean's list for the fall and spring semesters of her freshman year. "She loves Regency College. This is her last week of classes, and exams are next week. She'll have a short break before the fall semester begins." Kate looked at her watch. "In fact, we're meeting her for lunch at one o'clock, and we have another stop to make first. We probably should get going."

"We should, as soon as I grab a few bundles of yarn," Vivi said, plucking merino cashmere yarn in shades of limoncello, green tea, and olive from the cubbies and walking to the cash register. "Maybe if I create a spectacular sweater in fall colors, I can forget about how hot it is right now."

Paige laughed. "Good luck with that."

Kate and Vivi left Once Upon a Yarn, and soon Vivi was navigating her blue Mini Cooper though the one-way streets in downtown Fort Worth with impressive finesse. Kate figured her friend's job as an event planner at the posh Hamilton Arms Hotel enabled her to know the city inside and out. Several minutes later, Vivi pulled into the hotel's parking garage, which was right in the heart of the cultural district. Kate unfolded her long legs and got out of the car. They had about two hours before meeting Vanessa at the Greenery Bistro.

They crossed West Seventh Avenue to cut through Barnett Park on the way to Cosmic Creations, one of Vivi's favorite galleries, with work from artisans from all over the country—glass, ceramics, pottery, metal, wood, and jewelry, including folk art, recycled art, and green art.

"What exactly are we looking for?" Kate brushed a damp lock of brown hair from her forehead and dabbed her brow with a tissue as she stepped under a shade tree in the park. She looked wistfully at Vivi's short haircut. Although her own hair was pulled back in a ponytail, it still felt hot on her neck. It was only 11 a.m., but already the sun was blistering and the heat radiating from the concrete sidewalk was stifling. *Will I ever get used to Texas summers?*

"The most bizarre but classy table centerpieces in the world." Vivi chuckled at Kate's raised eyebrows. "Don't look at me. Those were bridezilla's exact words. I think she expected me to fly to Morocco and check out the open-air markets until I told her she'd have to pay my travel expenses. Then she said she'd settle for original pieces made by local artists."

"Roses in square vases won't cut it, huh?" Kate fanned herself with a notepad she'd taken from her purse.

"She doesn't even want the containers to match, much

less the flowers. But I know Cosmic Creations will have most of what I need for the perfect centerpieces."

"I see," Kate said, although she didn't understand that kind of extravagance. "Her parents probably wish she'd elope."

Vivi laughed as they crossed the street to Cosmic Creations. The gallery was nestled between a sushi bar and an upscale coffee shop. Kate stood in the doorway and looked in awe at the colorful array of wares. Would they have enough time to browse downstairs and take a peek up the spiral staircase to the second floor? She watched Vivi flit around the gallery for nearly two hours, approaching her selection in much the same manner as Kate did with her own designs—melding shapes, colors, textures, and patterns as she created the desired effect.

From time to time, Vivi snapped photos of items and texted them to the bride. Kate was surprised the bridezilla reacted favorably to the photos. By the time they approached the sales clerk, Vivi had chosen a variety of carved earth-toned gourd bowls, wood beads in vibrant colors, and coordinating miniature hand-woven cloths.

"I'll pull all of this together with dried flowers, grasses, and tea lights," Vivi explained to Kate as she handed her company credit card to the salesclerk.

"You're really good at what you do. I can't imagine how difficult it must be to work with difficult brides and their picky mothers." Kate stared at the pile of items by the register. "I can't wait to see the finished product."

"Thankfully, weddings are only a small part of what I do, and not all brides are this way. Most of them are delightfully excited. I love my job." Vivi looked at the clerk. "If you'll box this up for me, I'll come back tomorrow to get it."

They left the gallery and strolled a block to the Greenery Bistro. Although Vanessa's college wasn't too far from where

Kate lived in Sage Hills, she'd not seen her daughter in about three weeks. She was trying to let Vanessa enjoy her college days without interfering. Luckily Vanessa was good about calling every few days, so the empty nest wasn't as bad as Kate had feared.

The bistro was bustling with the lunchtime crowd. Kate and Vivi stood a few paces inside the door and scanned the room. Kate pointed to a slender young woman with long wavy hair gesturing to them from a table along a wall-length mural of a lush formal garden. "There's Vanessa."

As soon as the two friends had wound their way through the tables to the wall, Vanessa jumped from her chair and wrapped her arms around her mother. "You look great, Mom! I can't believe you have a tan!"

Kate stepped back, grinned, and nodded at Vivi. "We sure did pick the best house in Sage Hills. Since moving across the street from Vivi, she's not only taught me how to navigate Fort Worth, but she's passed along her gardening tips and shared her secret to staying in the sun without burning."

"Whatever you're doing, keep it up. Your skin has a healthy glow. Just remember to wear sun protection." Vanessa motioned for Kate and Vivi to sit. "You know, I was worried you might have a hard time adjusting to Texas without your Stony Point friends and the empty-nest thing. But you two seem to stay busy."

Before Kate or Vivi could reply, a waiter in a Hawaiian shirt arrived with menus to take their drink orders. "Our cranberry-hibiscus iced tea *is* outstanding." He smiled. "Would you like to try it?"

Vivi looked across the table at Kate and Vanessa. "The cranberry-hibiscus tea here *is* refreshing. Give it a whirl." When they nodded, Vivi looked at the waiter. "Three please."

Vanessa had just finished telling Kate and Vivi about preparing for the finals in her two classes—Survey of Mass

Communications and Weight Lifting—when the waiter returned with their tea. "Are you ready to order?"

"You can't go wrong with anything on this menu." Vivi pointed to the turkey club wrap listing. "I'll take this, but I'd like Gouda in place of provolone cheese."

Kate opted for the grilled-shrimp salad, and Vanessa ordered a blackened chicken sandwich. The waiter repeated their orders before disappearing in the crowd.

"So, Mom, what's new with Peter?" Vanessa stirred her tea with her straw and grinned before taking a long sip.

Kate shifted uncomfortably in her seat, unsure of what to say. Nothing was really new. She'd met Detective Peter Matthews when she attended a needlecraft conference in Fort Worth long before moving to Texas. Kate shuddered at the memory of meeting Peter after a man had been murdered during the conference. She'd been a suspect, and it had been a scary situation. Luckily, it hadn't taken Peter long to realize she couldn't have killed anyone. Instead of arresting her, he asked her for a date, and they went out once before she went back home to Maine. She hadn't told Peter in advance about her move to Texas, but they were reunited soon after her return when she'd been at the scene of another murder. His charmingly lopsided grin and dark blue eyes still made her heart quicken.

She cleared her throat. "Peter and I keep bumping into each other. We've been out a few times, but nothing serious." Kate stared into her glass. "He teases me a lot, but I enjoy his sense of humor."

Vivi's eyes danced as her laugh filtered across the table. "Don't let her fool you. The man is utterly smitten."

Vanessa cut her eyes from Vivi to Kate. "Mom, it really is OK with me if you date. I hope you find somebody special. You deserve it."

"That's what *I* keep telling her." Vivi looked at Vanessa. "Maybe one day she'll believe us."

"Can we change the subject, please?" Kate sighed. "I'd rather hear about the cute guy Vanessa met in her weight lifting class this semester."

Kate was relieved when Vanessa launched into a comedic retelling of the attractive, auburn-haired junior, Matt, who watched her complete a set of butterfly reps on a weight machine and felt the need to smugly correct her form. Vanessa, who'd spent time weight lifting as a star volleyball player in high school, had turned the tables on him and critiqued his squats with equal pretension. "When I recited the rules of form, the look on his face was classic. He apologized, and we've been friends ever since."

"So, is this relationship based on competition to see who has the best weight lifting form?" Vivi asked.

Vanessa laughed. "Yes, but it's all in fun. He really is a good guy."

They were still chuckling when the waiter arrived with their food and asked if they needed anything before he turned to the next table. Conversation was light and fun as the women enjoyed their lunch.

"Vivi and I are going to do a bit of window shopping after lunch so I can get more familiar with the area." Kate took a swig of tea. "Do you have time to go with us? We won't take long."

Vanessa took out her smartphone and scrolled through it. "I have an hour or so. I'd love to spend it with you."

Eclectic shops, cafés, and nightclubs became more plentiful as Kate, Vanessa, and Vivi strolled closer to the downtown area.

They paused frequently to check out window dressings—the latest fashions, menus featuring nouvelle cuisine, best-selling books, dance-class schedules, antiques, and marquees for upcoming band performances.

Kate and Vivi watched as Vanessa walked ahead of them to the entrance of what appeared to be a music hall in the basement of an old department store.

"She's a beautiful young woman, Kate." Vivi looked at her friend. "Witty and intelligent. You've done a great job raising her."

Kate smiled and joy filled her. "She *is* amazing, isn't she? In spite of her father's alcoholic ramblings and the tension at home before the divorce, Vanessa is happy, grounded, and confident. I'm so proud of her."

"Mom, look at this!" Vanessa's head bobbed with excitement as she motioned them closer to Charley's Jazz Room with one hand and pointed to a marquee with the other.

Kate and Vivi picked up their pace. Kate froze when she gazed at the marquee. *It can't be.*

"Is this *our* Cole Cutchins? Look, he's performing here on Saturday!" Vanessa squealed. You haven't seen him in a while. You should go. I'd go if I didn't have finals to study for."

A thrill ran through Kate's body. She'd recognize those hazel eyes anywhere. Her heart skipped a beat. "Yes, that's Cole. I can't believe it. The last time we talked was months before we moved. He said then that his band had a new member and there were plans for a six-state tour in the works."

"So, who is this gorgeous man with the intense eyes and sweet smile?" Vivi stared at the poster. "I always did have a thing for blond hair. Did Vanessa say he's yours?"

Kate was still reeling from seeing Cole's face, even in a poster, after all this time. "No, he isn't really mine. I just met him at a jazz club in New York when I went to a fiber arts convention with a couple of friends from Stony Point. We were chasing down the identity of a jazz singer, and we ended up at the club where he plays regularly."

Vanessa put her arm around her mother's shoulders. "Don't sell yourself short." She looked at Vivi. "Cole liked Mom so much that he not only visited her in Stony Point, but he composed a beautiful song for her too. He sings and plays the trumpet."

Vivi's eyes widened. "You have your own song?"

"Yes." Kate felt her face reddening. "It's beautiful."

Vanessa grinned. "He named it *Truly Kate*. Isn't that romantic?"

"It sure is! What are we waiting for?" Vivi stepped to the door and tugged. "Let's get tickets for his show."

Two

"Can you believe I've worked in downtown Fort Worth for ten years and I've never been inside this place?" Vivi's eyes darted from one end of Charley's Jazz Room to the other while she and Kate waited for Cole's performance to begin. "It's really cool."

Kate nodded. "I'm glad we arrived early enough to get a table close to the front." Their table was in the second row, close to the wall to the left of the stage, giving them a good view of the stage and the tables behind them. Vivi's reaction to Charley's reminded Kate of her own excitement when she was first exposed to the jazz scene at the Avant-Garde, the club in New York City where she'd met Cole. Not much of a drinker, she'd been unsure of how she'd like the atmosphere. She hadn't known what to expect of the music, either. Kate had been surprised at how the atmosphere had enveloped her and the music had touched her soul.

"Aren't you bursting with anticipation to see Cole again? I know I would be." Vivi stirred the ice in her tall glass with vigor.

"More nervous than anything, I think. But I'm excited too." Kate glanced at her watch. *Fifteen minutes until showtime.* "I have no idea how he will react to seeing me."

Charley's had the same feel as the Avant-Garde—laid-back but crackling with creative sparks. *Cole must love this place,* looking around at the light walls spruced up with rich wood accents and art deco curves. A deep red curtain lent a luxurious backdrop to the stage, and matching tiebacks marked the entries into two small alcoves with table seating on either side of the stage. A bar filled half of the wall on the other side of the room opposite Kate and Vivi's table. The lights were low and votive candles flickered on each table. A few framed black-and-white photos of past performers dotted the walls, but folks obviously didn't come here for artwork; they came for the music.

Their server, who had introduced herself earlier as Bonnie, now approached their table, carrying an empty tray. "Would you like to order another drink? The show will be starting soon."

"That would be great." Vivi rummaged through her purse, pulled out a pen, scribbled a note on her napkin, and gave it to the server. "Would you please give this to Cole Cutchins?"

Bonnie read the note silently. "Are you Kate?" she asked Vivi.

"No, I am." Kate's eyes widened, and she looked at Vivi. "What did you do?"

"Nothing bad. I just told him that Kate Stevens was in the audience and would like to see him." Vivi batted her eyelashes. "That's OK, isn't it?"

Bonnie cleared her throat and looked at Kate. "Do you want me to give this to him?"

Several seconds passed before Kate spoke. "Yes, thank you. I'd like him to know I'm here."

Just as Bonnie stepped to the next table, the stage lights came on and a gray-haired man stepped into the spotlight. "Welcome to Charley's. I'm Duke Richards. Charley was my dad. My family has been providing the very best in jazz music to Fort Worth for more than fifty years. Tonight we bring you a crowd favorite, returning to Charley's on the heels of cutting their new CD of original music, *Hot and Cole*. Give it up for Cole Cutchins and his band."

Cole stepped out, and Kate caught her breath. He was

still gorgeous. She felt her heart pick up the pace with the music of Cole's first number. Memories of her visit to New York and his to Stony Point flickered through her mind. He'd been easy to talk to, and he made her laugh. *Why didn't we keep in touch?* Kate sipped her soda, her eyes glued on Cole. *Because after my disastrous marriage to Harry, I was afraid to trust another man.*

Vivi tugged on the sleeve of her blouse. Kate felt Vivi's breath on her ear. "So, is he still as handsome and talented as you remember?"

"Uh-huh."

"Is he going to be competition for our favorite detective?"

"They'll kick you out if you talk during the show," Kate whispered. She turned her attention back to the stage, and they listened without talking through the rest of the set. When the band announced their break and filed offstage, Kate wondered if Bonnie had given Vivi's note to Cole. Would he want to see her after all this time?

The house lights brightened a bit, and conversations began to buzz around the room. Kate glanced at the backstage door repeatedly as she and Vivi chatted about music. Her friend was bent on turning Kate into a country music fan.

"Well, if it isn't the amateur sleuths. I had no idea you two were into jazz music."

Kate looked up and found Peter's dark blue eyes sparkling down at her. "Hi, Peter. And I might say the same about you. I thought you were a country-western type of guy."

"I am. But several guys from the force wanted to listen to some jazz tonight, so I thought I'd tag along." He looked from Kate to Vivi. "I didn't expect to see you two here."

"If you must know, we're here with the band." Vivi flashed a mischievous smile at Peter. "Kate knows the trumpet player."

He arched an eyebrow. "With the band, huh?"

Kate hoped Cole wouldn't choose that moment to make an appearance at their table. "Well, I met Cole at a jazz club during a trip to New York City. We stayed in touch for a while. When I found out he was playing here, I thought I'd catch the show."

She couldn't help noticing how attractive Peter looked in his casual brown suit and yellow shirt. He couldn't quite give up his cowboy style; his trusty Western boots peeked out from his pants leg. He ran a hand through his unruly hair and glanced at the stage, sighing when he returned his gaze to Kate.

"I guess if you're playing groupie, then this isn't the best time to ask you out to dinner." He flashed a lopsided smile. "But this doesn't mean I'm giving up."

His words thrilled Kate. As leery as she was about getting too attached to any man, she was glad to have Peter in her life. She wasn't sure how to respond to his comment.

"Good. *Don't* give up," Vivi piped up. "Just remember you're not only competing with a musician, but with a man who wrote a song just for Kate."

Peter's eyes widened. "You're his muse?" He smiled. "That's not surprising."

Kate was ready to change the subject but was rescued from responding when the lights dimmed. Peter returned to his table, and the band returned to the stage. During the applause, Vivi leaned over and tapped Kate's shoulder. "Are you too disappointed Cole didn't come by during the break?"

"Sort of." Kate shrugged. She was both relieved and disappointed. "It would have been uncomfortable talking to Peter and Cole at the same time. But still, why didn't he stop by? Maybe he doesn't want to see me."

"I don't know, but look at the stage." Vivi placed a hand on Kate's forearm. "Maybe that explains it."

Kate looked up just in time to see their server hand Cole a napkin and gesture toward their table. Kate's heart started beating faster. "He didn't know we were here!"

"Sure looks like it." Vivi smiled. "Now we can enjoy the show. I must admit, I kinda like this music."

Kate's head bobbed to the opening tune. She'd been so busy lately that she'd forgotten how much she enjoyed listening to jazz.

As the notes faded from Miles Davis's *All Blues*, an angry yell pierced the air. "You think you're so talented and successful, Cole Cutchins!"

The room fell silent as an emaciated man with stringy, shoulder-length brown hair jumped up and shook his fist at the startled front man. "But you're nothing but a traitor and cutthroat musician! You ruin people!"

Cole's mouth fell open, and his eyes widened as the man continued to shout epithets and gesture at him. A man—probably the band's manager, Kate thought—leaped onstage and herded the musicians off stage right. People at nearby tables scooted their seats farther away from the heckler. Several folks moved out of the way as club employees subdued the man.

Like everyone else, Kate was stunned. She watched the scene unfold as if she were in a movie theater instead of a jazz club.

"Wow." Vivi's voice pulled Kate from her daze. "Is it possible you don't know Cole as well as you thought?"

Kate wondered the same thing but quickly nixed the idea. "He's won awards for teaching and promoting musicians. He's also been recognized for his community service. I just can't see him as a cutthroat."

"This night sure is getting interesting, and here I thought this would be a boring evening of dull jazz music." Vivi's eyes shifted toward the three men surrounding the heckler, who had calmed down enough to have a conversation. "I guess I was wrong."

"Seems so," Kate said, her eyes glued to the crowd in the center of the room. "I wonder if the band will finish the set."

After the man was escorted from the building by a surly bouncer, Cole's band returned to the stage and played two original instrumental pieces before he slid the bell of his trumpet onto the instrument stand, took a swig of water from a glass resting on a nearby Parsons table, and stepped to the microphone. "I'm often asked where inspiration for my original melodies comes from. Sometimes I don't have a true answer; the song just echoes through my head." Cole paused and cleared his throat. "Once in a while, something or someone moves me to compose. This next song is one of the latter. It was written for a beautiful, graceful, and talented woman I met in New York about three years ago. At the break, I learned she's in the audience tonight. Our last song of the night is *Truly Kate*."

"Woo-hoo!" Vivi clapped although most of the room was quiet.

Kate felt warmth travel from her neck to the top of her head as Cole looked toward their table and smiled. "Shush, Vivi. Please," Kate whispered. "There's already enough attention focused on me right now."

Cool trumpeter Cole placed the horn to his lips, and an ethereal melody filled the room. During his brief rests when the other members of the band played, he made eye contact with several people in the audience, but his gaze always returned to Kate. She couldn't help but smile. Not every woman was lucky enough to have a song written for her. *Truly Kate* was breathtakingly beautiful. Kate wondered how she could ever measure up to the song.

As soon as the music faded away, Vivi put her lips to Kate's ear. "The music makes you sound like an angel."

"I'm not so sure how angelic I was when we met."

"How's that?"

"I was returning to my seat with a drink during the band's break, and I bumped into him. My drink spilled down the front of his shirt." Kate pushed her glass away. "Notice I didn't order anything at the bar tonight. I waited patiently for the server to come to us."

"You really did that?" Vivi giggled. "I guess that was one way to get his attention."

"Yes, I really did, and I was mortified." Kate shook her head and smiled. "I felt like such a klutz, but he was sweet about it."

Vivi laughed. "Don't look now, but here he comes."

Kate looked up just as Cole reached the table. "Hi, Kate." He bent down and kissed her cheek. "I wish your server had given me the note before it was time to start the last set." Cole smiled warmly. "It's great to see you. May I sit?"

"Sure. I'm happy to see you too, Cole." Kate turned her head to Vivi. "This is my friend, Vivi Lawrence. She's been a godsend, helping me get acclimated to the Fort Worth area."

After shaking hands with Vivi, Cole put his elbows on the table and leaned toward Kate. "I didn't realize you'd already moved. How long have you been here?"

"Nearly a year. Vanessa begins her sophomore year at Regency College in a few weeks." Kate couldn't stop looking at Cole's eyes. "How've you been?"

"Busy. Teaching, writing, recording, performing. We're

almost at the end of our tour." Cole put a hand over Kate's. "I'd love to take you both out for coffee so we can catch up. I just need to pack up my equipment first."

Kate glanced at her watch. By the time Cole finished at the club, it would probably be close to eleven o'clock. "I need to be up early for church in the morning. Could we meet for lunch tomorrow instead?"

"Sure. Where and when?"

Kate pulled her purse from beneath the table and retrieved her business card case and a pen from the side pocket. She removed a card and returned the case to her purse. Looking at the card, she chuckled. "I seem to be out of my cards, but here's one of Vivi's." She scribbled the name and location of her favorite lunch spot in Sage Hills on the back before handing it to Cole. "Will two o'clock work? That will give me plenty of time to get back after church and get a few things done before lunch."

"That'll be fine." Cole smiled. "Looking forward to it."

"I hope I'm not interrupting anything." Peter had walked up, a few of his police buddies behind him.

Kate looked up when she heard Peter's voice and wondered how long he'd been standing there. Judging from the look on his face, he must have heard her making lunch plans with Cole. She glanced back at Cole, who was studying Peter with interest.

"I'm Cole Cutchins." Cole extended his hand to Peter. "We're just catching up. I haven't seen Kate in a long time."

Peter shook the proffered hand, his eyes assessing the musician. "Just catching up, huh? Nice song, by the way. Kate *is* pretty special."

"Yes, she is. And thank you. Kate's song is a crowd favorite. It's been a hit download on iTunes."

Peter's buddies spread out to surround Cole, two on one side and two behind him. An alarm went off inside Kate. They were trying to intimidate Cole, just like her ex-husband had intimidated her with raised voices, aggression, and input from his drinking buddies.

"Do you write songs for all the women you meet in clubs? You must have a woman in every town you've played." Peter used his interrogation voice, and Kate flinched. She'd been on the receiving end of that voice a few times.

Kate pushed her chair back from the table and put her purse strap on her shoulder. "Vivi, I'm ready to go, are you?" When Vivi nodded, Kate looked at Cole. "Thank you for playing my song. I'm looking forward to seeing you tomorrow."

She faced Peter. "Good night, Peter. I hope you and your friends enjoyed your evening."

Kate grabbed Vivi's elbow and steered her toward the door. Vivi quickly called out her goodbyes over her shoulder. When they stepped onto the sidewalk outside the club, Kate closed her eyes, drew in a long breath, and held it a moment before exhaling. She stood motionless as she tried to make sense of the evening.

"What was *that* all about?" Kate asked.

"Well, hon, it seems to me that those two gorgeous men were vying for your affection," Vivi replied.

Kate closed her eyes and shook her head. "I never thought I'd see the day."

Vivi put her arm around Kate and gave her a squeeze as they walked toward the car. "Get used to it. I have a feeling your favorite detective doesn't like competition."

Three

"Through many dangers, toils and snares, I have already come; 'Tis grace hath brought me safe thus far, and grace will lead me home." Kate drummed her fingers on the van's steering wheel and sang the lyrics to her favorite hymn, *Amazing Grace*, trying to imitate the folksy Southern accent of the vocalist who had sung in church earlier that morning. His upbeat tempo and the song's hopeful words helped ease the tension she'd felt since leaving Charley's Jazz Room.

Kate had almost skipped church. Tired from being out late the previous night and still reeling from watching two men compete for her attention, Kate had been tempted to stay home and rest. She needed to figure out how she felt about seeing Cole again. But she felt compelled to go to the small, homey community church in Sage Hills despite—or maybe because of—her frame of mind. Now, as she turned onto Hawkins Drive toward her home, she was feeling vibrant and thankful.

That changed when she got home and found a tan Ford Taurus, Peter's unmarked police car, in front of it. By the time she'd pulled into the driveway and parked, a concerned-looking Peter was standing nearby, waiting for her to get out of the van. Was he irritated with her for making a lunch date with Cole last night? Surely not. She and Peter were barely past being friends. They'd been on a few dates, but they had shared only one goodnight kiss. Yet, it was awfully early for a Sunday visit, and he didn't look very happy. Taking a deep breath, she opened her car door. "Good morning, Peter." She tried to sound cheery, but the words didn't come out that way. Kate slid off the seat and closed the door behind her. He didn't respond, so she felt the need to keep talking. "I went to the early church service this morning." Kate hesitated. What should she say next? "Would you like some coffee?"

He finally gave her a small smile. "Coffee would be good, but this isn't a social call."

Peter had shown up at Kate's house on department business several times over the past year when she was embroiled in one mystery or another. Kate raised her eyebrows. "I wondered when I saw you weren't in your truck. What's up?"

"I'll tell you while the coffee's brewing." Peter followed Kate through the patio and stood by the back door as she unlocked it.

"You sound awfully mysterious," Kate said, walking into the kitchen and setting her purse on the end chair. When he responded by silently taking a seat at the table, she scooped coffee from the canister into the filter and poured water through the coffeemaker. After setting two mugs, a pair of spoons, and a pitcher of milk on the counter, Kate sat down in the chair opposite Peter. "Now, tell me what this is all about."

Peter looked her in the eyes. "Where is your friend Cole?"

Kate stared right back at him. "I haven't seen him since I left the club last night, but I'm listening if you're ready to apologize for the childish intimidation tactics you and your friends used to try to drive him away." Peter blinked first and lowered his eyes. "Cole is none of your business," she said.

"But you see, I'm afraid he is," Peter said, looking up again. "The man who disrupted his show was found dead in the alley last night. That makes Cole a person of interest in a possible murder investigation and very much my business."

Kate sat in silence until the coffeepot sputtered. She rose and poured two cups of coffee, adding a splash of milk to hers. After placing the mug of black coffee in front of Peter, she sat back down in front of him. "Maybe you need to start from the beginning."

Peter flipped his notebook open and glanced down at the page before looking at Kate. "Brice Denman, the man who yelled at Cole during his show, was found dead by a club employee who was taking out the trash sometime after midnight." Peter sipped his coffee. "Evidently, this employee had made several trips to the Dumpster. During an earlier trip, he saw Cole in the alley, arguing with Denman. Cole may have been the last person to see Denman alive, so I need to talk to him. But he didn't stay with the band in the hotel suite, and nobody seems to know where he is. Looks suspicious to me."

Kate shook her head. "You can't possibly think Cole has anything to do with this. He's a respected music professor at Columbia University." Kate took a deep breath. "He's a musician, not a killer."

"The two aren't mutually exclusive, Kate. How well do you really know him, anyway?" Peter let his words sink in. "Did you do any kind of background check?"

"No," Kate said. "I'm not in the habit of investigating everyone I know."

"You can be naive, Kate. Sometimes you trust too easily." Peter rubbed his chin and stared at her.

Kate leaned forward and placed her hands on the table. "My level of trust is irrelevant at the moment. I have nothing to do with this. What do you want from me?"

"I want you to tell me where to find your friend Cole."

Kate stood and paced across the kitchen. He'd called her naive and talked to her like she was a child. Is that what he really thought of her? She counted to ten to keep calm and returned to her seat. "Peter, I really don't know where Cole is. I haven't heard from him since I left the club." She glanced at the digital clock on the stove. It was eleven thirty. "But we're meeting for lunch at two o'clock at the Hilltop Restaurant in Sage Hills."

Peter scribbled in his notebook. "I'd rather you not go to lunch with Cole." Kate took a deep breath and opened her mouth to reply, but Peter held up his hand to silence her. "But if he's not located before your meeting, it might be the best time for him to be questioned." He put his hand down. "I trust you to not let him know this."

Kate's heart sank. "You want me to set him up? To let him think we are really having lunch, only to find you waiting there for him?"

Peter stood up and walked around the table to Kate. "Only if we don't find him first. Call me if you hear from him before your lunch date."

She nodded. "I don't expect to hear from him, but OK."

Peter stepped closer, his eyes fixed on hers. Kate's heart rate skyrocketed. Was Peter going to kiss her after such a strange conversation? But instead, Peter fished a small canister out of his pants pocket and handed it to Kate. Kate saw it was Mace.

"You're important to me, so please be careful." He took Kate's hand, placed the canister of Mace in her palm, and closed her fingers around it. "I'd feel better if you had some sort of protection. Your friend is a person of interest in a murder investigation." He squeezed her hand, let it go, and strode to the door before he turned around. "I'll call you. Keep your phone handy." Then he was gone.

Kate stood unmoving for a minute and tried to make sense of the conversation and her own feelings. Peter seemed to believe Cole was capable of murder. Was that even remotely possible? Or was Peter not willing to consider another suspect? He'd certainly seemed jealous at the club. "Stop it, Kate." Her words echoed through the kitchen. "Peter is a professional. He wouldn't jeopardize his career over petty jealousy."

She poured another cup of coffee and carried it to her design studio. Perhaps sketching a new design for Paige to display at Once Upon a Yarn would keep her mind off the murder until it was time to meet Cole for lunch. She'd wanted to experiment with designs for a sheer-sleeved, floral-lace shirt in white that could be worn to dress up jeans or paired with a fancy skirt, but she couldn't seem to find time. *The time is now*, she decided. She sketched out the basic shape of the shirt—formfitting sleeves, a scoop neck, and a scalloped tail. She was just starting to play with floral designs to see which combinations worked best when her cellphone rang in the kitchen. She ran down the hall to get it and smiled when she saw Vanessa's number on the caller ID.

"Hi, Vanessa. How are you?" Kate padded into the living room and curled up on the sofa.

"Hi, Mom. I just called to find out how the concert went. How did Cole react when you saw him? Was he surprised?"

"It was a pretty surprising night all around, I'd say."

"How so?" Vanessa asked. "I always liked Cole. He took time to play at that fundraiser back in Maine and didn't even charge us. He's a good guy."

Kate wasn't sure if she should first tell Vanessa about Cole's performance or start with Peter's morning visit. She opted to tell her about the night at the club first, including the incident with the heckler.

When she finished, Vanessa whistled. "Mom! You had two guys almost fighting over you? What did you do?"

"Well, first I made a lunch date with Cole for today. Then Vivi and I dashed out of Charley's before Peter could say much about it."

"Good call." Vanessa chuckled. "What time is your lunch?"

Kate bit her lip. "In about forty-five minutes, but I'm not sure if I should still go."

"Why not? It sounds like you didn't have much of a chance to talk last night."

"It seems there was a murder last night outside the club." Kate repeated the information Peter had told her earlier. Kate could hardly believe she was talking about Cole and murder in the same conversation.

"What are you going to do?" Vanessa sounded concerned.

"I haven't heard back from Peter yet. He doesn't want me to go unless he can't find Cole before I'm supposed to meet him," Kate explained. "If he hasn't found him, then Peter wants me to keep the meeting so he can show up. But I think I want to see Cole and hear what he has to say whether or not Peter calls."

"This is some pretty serious stuff, Mom."

"To tell you the truth, I have mixed feelings about Cole, taking out of the equation that he might be connected to a murder. We've had some fun together, but we've spent so much time apart that it seems I hardly know him. On the other hand, I'm not too happy with how Peter acted at the club. I'm not sure if he was jealous or being overprotective, but he made me feel uneasy." She sighed. "I feel so conflicted."

"Do you want me to come over?"

"No, you need to study for your finals. I'll be fine," Kate said, hoping her voice sounded positive. "I'll call as soon as I have anything new to report."

"I'll hold you to that. I'll be waiting to hear about what happens." Vanessa cleared her throat. "I love you. Please be careful."

"I will. I love you too." Kate disconnected the call and placed her phone on the cushion beside her.

The house was quiet. Kate leaned into the sofa and closed her eyes. It was decision time. Should she wait to hear from Peter or head to the Hilltop Restaurant? After several minutes, she stood up, straightened the tail of her lavender sweater over her white skirt, went into the kitchen to grab her purse and keys, and left through the back door.

Four

Kate gazed out the window of the Hilltop Restaurant, her eyes following the slope of the hill to the bottom, where a dozen mallard ducks were leisurely paddling around the small pond. Benches and shade trees provided respite for restaurant patrons wishing to stroll through the park. Would she and Cole have the opportunity to visit the ducks after lunch, or would Peter disrupt their meal?

She glanced at her watch. It was 2:10; Cole was ten minutes late. Had Peter found him and detained him at the police station?

"Is this seat taken?" Cole's eyes twinkled down at her, and he bent to kiss her cheek, keeping one arm behind him. "I'm sorry I'm late. I took a wrong turn coming out of Fort Worth."

"This seat has your name on it." Kate gestured toward the empty chair with a flourish.

Cole sat down. "I'm glad we have a chance to catch up." He gazed at her and smiled. "It's great to see you, Kate."

Kate nodded, her reply cut off by the arrival of their server, a tall young woman. After introducing herself as Clarisse, she handed them menus and took their drink order before giving the couple another chance to talk.

"Cole, have you heard from Detective Matthews? He was—"

"He was pretty possessive of you last night, so I'd rather not talk about him." Cole stared into her eyes. "Texas agrees with you, Kate. You look radiant." Cole sounded wistful. "I wish we could have seen each other before you moved."

Kate sighed. Should she try to tell Cole about Peter's visit or carry on as if nothing happened, especially since Peter hadn't shown up at the restaurant? She looked at her watch. It was now more than thirty minutes past the time she'd told Peter she'd be meeting Cole. Maybe Peter had caught the real killer, and Cole was off the hook.

"It's been a good change for me." She pulled her business card case from her purse, removed a card, and handed it to Cole. "I replenished my supply since last night." She smiled and paused before continuing. "Since I arrived, I've found an agent and a publisher, and my designs are selling well locally and through my website."

Cole stared at the card and grinned. "I knew you'd be successful. You deserve it."

"The best part is Vanessa loves college life at Regency. I'm blessed. Although she studies long hours, keeps an active social life, and works part-time in the campus bookstore, Vanessa still finds time to call regularly and meet in the city from time to time." Kate paused as the server returned with their water and iced tea, mentioned the lunch special of grilled wild salmon with capers, and asked them if they were ready to order.

"The salmon sounds great to me." Kate reached for her water.

Clarisse looked at Cole. "Do you need a minute?"

"No, I'll have the salmon as well." Cole handed her the menus.

"The salmon is always good here. You'll enjoy it," Kate said as the server walked away. "So, how have *you* been? Still balancing teaching and touring?"

"And recording," Cole added. He pulled a thin square package from his lap and slid it across the table. "We cut a new album earlier this year. *Truly Kate* is on there. It's gotten some airplay on jazz radio in New York and favorable reviews from the critics."

Kate's fingers brushed Cole's as she reached for the CD, and the touch was electric. He'd recorded her song! He thought of her even though they'd been out of touch. She smiled. *Peter must be wrong about him.* Cole seemed so sincere. How in the world could he be involved in a murder?

"Thank you, for the song and the CD." Kate looked at the CD and inhaled deeply. The artwork featured a profile of a man and a woman staring at a trumpet between them. Kate was sure the profile was hers. "I'm honored that you—"

"Well, if it isn't Cole Cutchins." A shadow hovered over the table. "I've been looking for you since around midnight last night."

Cole narrowed his eyes and glanced from Kate to Peter. "You must have some deep-seated jealousy issues. We're just having lunch."

Peter pulled a chair from a neighboring table and sat between Cole and Kate. "I'd like to talk to you about Brice Denman and his disruption during your show last night."

Cole shook his head as if his mind were shifting gears. "Brice is an unfortunate lost cause. It's a shame, really, because he was a brilliant musician until drugs took over his life. He squandered his talent and money on cocaine."

He stopped talking as Clarisse arrived holding trays laden with salmon, wild rice, and grilled vegetables. After she arranged the food on the table, she turned to Peter. "Would you like to order lunch?"

Peter declined and waited until Clarisse had moved on. "How long had it been since you'd seen him last?"

"About two and a half or three years." Cole stuck his fork in the salmon fillet. "Look, could we discuss Brice after we finish lunch? You're making me lose my appetite."

"Oh? Why is that?" Peter's eyes didn't leave Cole's face.

"It's not a pretty story." Cole put his fork down on his plate. "Brice was one of the most talented musicians I'd ever worked with—vocals, drums, piano. But he began missing rehearsals and performances. Eventually, he hocked his equipment and most of his instruments. In the end, his inconsistency cost us a couple of high-paying gigs. I told him to get his act together and kick the habit because we couldn't risk our reputation on his addiction."

"Anything else?"

"No. I told you. I haven't seen him in years," said Cole, raising his voice. "Obviously he has issues with me."

Kate cleared her throat. "Peter, you're causing a scene. Would you please let us finish our lunch and then continue this outside?"

"Kate, you know I can't do that," Peter said. "This can't wait."

Cole pushed his chair back and stood up. "Then why don't you tell me what this is all about?"

Peter stood and looked Cole in the eye. "You were seen arguing with Denman after the show. Then Denman turns up dead in the alley, and you're nowhere to be found. Why don't you explain that to me?"

Cole's mouth fell open, his eyes closing as he shook his head. "Brice is dead? Did he OD? He was definitely agitated last night. He could have been on something."

"You tell me. You're the one who was seen with him after the show." Peter's voice grew louder.

Kate cringed but was relieved when she saw Clarisse approach them. She stood up and stepped away from the table. "May we have our check please? We need to leave."

The server glanced at the two men glaring at each other before looking at the nearly full plates on the table. "Certainly. Would you like to-go boxes?" Kate shook her head, and Clarisse turned on her heel and dashed to the register area.

"Can we please take this outside? People are starting to stare." Kate brushed Cole's arm. "I'll wait for the check. You two go on outside, and I'll meet you there."

Cole took his wallet from his back pocket, opened it, retrieved several bills, and tossed them on the table. "This should more than cover it. Let's go."

The trio strode through the restaurant and nearly collided with Clarisse on their way to the door. Assuring her that the payment was on the table, Kate led the way outside, then down the grassy slope to a pair of secluded benches near the pond. Kate and Cole sat down on the bench facing the water. Peter stood in front of the opposite bench, facing them.

Looking up at Peter towering over them, Kate spoke first. "Peter, please sit down. He'll answer your questions." Her voice was strong and controlled, opposite the heartbeat pounding on her ribcage. She inhaled a deep breath and slowly let it out as Peter sat. "Thank you."

Pulling a small pad and pen from his shirt pocket, Peter resumed the interrogation. "We'll start with what happened between you and Denman as you left the club last night."

Cole winced. "When I walked into the alley to put my gear in the van, Brice was waiting for me, yelling garbage similar to what he'd shouted in the club. I tried to reason with him, to calm him down. I wanted him to know I never doubted his talent as a musician, and it was the addiction that took his career away, not me or the band." Cole paused and glanced toward the water. "When it was clear he wouldn't listen, I started to walk away, but then he pulled a gun and waved it in my face saying he was going to kill me for ruining him."

Before she could stop herself, Kate gasped. "A gun? What did you do?"

"Kate, I'll ask the questions, OK?" Peter's tone softened. "I know it's difficult."

"I'm OK. I'll be quiet." Kate nodded. "Go on."

"Cole, what happened after Denman began waving the gun?" Peter's voice was stern.

"I reacted instinctively and grabbed for the gun. It seemed like it took forever to get it, but finally I managed to knock it out of his hand. It skidded away, and I took the opportunity to jump into the van and pull it around to the front of the club so we could finish loading there. Most of the patrons were gone by that time."

"And then what did you do?"

"I drove back to the hotel with the band."

Peter flipped a page in his notebook. "But you didn't stay there. Where were you?"

"I dropped off the guys and drove around, looking for Brice. As scary as it was having a gun pointed at me, I didn't like leaving things that way. After all, we were friends at one time. I felt like I should have tried harder to help him before sending him packing."

Peter lifted his eyes from the notebook. "Did you take anyone with you?"

"No. I went alone. I was the one who set Brice off; it was my responsibility to find him. And I was the only one who hadn't been drinking before we left the club."

"Where did you go?"

Cole unhooked his smartphone from his belt and punched several keys. "It'll be easier to show you." A few seconds later he held the phone out to Peter.

"Cemeteries?" Peter's eyebrows furrowed as he scrolled down the list. "Why?"

"It's creepy, I know. But when we performed in New York

City together, Brice's way to unwind after a show was to find the nearest cemetery. Then he would get high and, in his words, commune with the dead. He'd sleep it off, and the caretaker or the cops would run him out of the graveyard in the morning." Cole shuddered. "I found this list of cemeteries and started looking through those closest to the club."

"There must be fifty listed here. Did you go to all of them?" Peter scribbled in his notebook and returned Cole's phone.

Cole shook his head. "Some of them were locked up, and I couldn't find a way in. I figured if the gates were too hard for me to climb, they'd be doubly so for Brice."

Kate sat in stunned silence. *Drugs? Cemeteries? Murder?* "I can't believe you did this all by yourself," she said.

"I can't believe you did it at all." Peter looked Cole in the eyes. "Can you tell me why Brice Denman was found near the Dumpster behind Charley's with a bullet in his chest after you were seen arguing with him in the alley?"

Cole's eyes widened, and he shook his head. "No. I can't answer that because Brice was alive when I left the alley."

Peter closed his notebook and stood up. "Would you be willing to come downtown with me to make a formal statement and provide a DNA sample and fingerprints?"

"Am I under arrest?"

"No."

Cole was silent a moment as they walked toward the parking lot. "I'd like to call my attorney."

"Be my guest."

Cole stepped away from Kate and Peter to make his call.

Peter watched his suspect for a few seconds before turning to Kate. "The media is already asking questions. Be prepared, and don't respond to any requests for interviews."

"I won't. Reporters make me nervous." Kate's gaze drifted

to Cole, who was pacing along the walkway. "Are you going to arrest Cole?"

"Not yet. We're still investigating. Just go home. Don't talk to anyone about this, and don't worry. We'll find out what really happened to Brice Denman."

"I know you will." Kate's smile was thin. "I hope it's soon."

Cole clipped his cellphone back onto his belt and joined Kate and Cole. "My attorney, Evan Kline, advised me to not give fingerprints or a DNA sample right now." He paused. "I'll cooperate with the investigation and answer any additional questions you have though."

Peter nodded and flipped through his pad, scanning his notes. "What is the best contact phone number for you?"

"My cellphone." Cole cleared his throat and recited the number.

"I'd appreciate it if you'd make yourself available for additional questions," said Peter, returning his pad and pen to his pocket.

"Anytime. I'll be here until our gig is over, in a couple of weeks. You know where to find me."

"Indeed," said Peter, his attention briefly captured by a green SUV entering the parking lot. "May I have a private word with Kate, please?"

"Sure. I'll head back to the hotel." Cole lightly squeezed Kate's hand and then walked to the parking lot and climbed into his van.

Peter tapped Kate's arm and tilted his head in the direction of the green SUV. "That belongs to a local newspaper reporter. Be careful. You're already on their radar."

Kate shuddered. "Thanks for the warning. I will."

Five

Kate stared at the television Monday morning as yet another photo of Cole was displayed next to a snapshot of Brice Denman on the *Fort Worth Early News*. "Didn't you say all there was to say about Cole yesterday? Everyone knows his complete background by now." She felt better saying the words aloud even though nobody was there to hear.

Cole hadn't been arrested. The previous night he'd called to say his attorney was clearing his schedule to fly to Texas, but in the meantime, he recommended Cole remain at the hotel to lay low. The morning news seemed to confirm this, but still reporters had hounded anyone connected to Cole to provide updates on Sunday's afternoon and evening newscasts.

"What a mess," she muttered, unable to take her eyes off the television.

The doorbell chimed, and Kate muted the TV with the remote before going to answer the door. Looking through the peephole, the lone dark-haired young woman looked vaguely familiar, but Kate couldn't see her features clearly. Kate opened the door, and the woman thrust a microphone in her face.

"Mrs. Stevens? I'm Trista Sheen with *Good Day Fort Worth*. I understand you're good friends with Cole Cutchins, a person of interest in the Brice Denman murder. Do you think he is capable of killing someone?" The reporter leaned forward. "We just learned from an anonymous source that Brice Denman was murdered with his own gun. What do you think happened Saturday night?"

Several bright flashes went off behind Trista Sheen, and Kate realized a line of reporters, photographers, and cameramen from several media outlets stood in her yard. *How did they find me? And when and how did they learn the gun had belonged to Brice? Peter didn't mention the gun owner.* She shook off the surprise and counted to ten before opening her mouth to speak. "I'm afraid I have nothing at all to say. No comment." She closed the door as reporters began shouting questions. Her mind was whirling. *Why are they dogging me? I had nothing to do with the killing.*

Grabbing her phone off the coffee table, Kate called Peter to see if there was any way to make the reporters leave. She exhaled with relief when he answered the phone. "Peter, I'm so glad you picked up. There's a crowd of reporters at my front door. How can I make them leave?"

"I was afraid they'd find you when the crime reporter from *The Fort Worth Post* showed up asking about the woman Cole dedicated the song to on the night of the murder. I imagine they found out about it from someone at the club." Peter paused. "I'll call Johnny Castille and see if anyone at Sage Hills PD can provide some crowd control. If I weren't tied up with the investigation, I'd stop by and handle it."

"Thank you. I'll appreciate anything you can do." Kate carried the phone to the window and peered through the mini blinds. "It looks like a couple of reporters have left, but a lot of them are still out there, just hanging around by their vehicles. It's unnerving."

"Sit tight and don't open the door unless it's Johnny or an officer who shows you his badge. Keep your blinds shut. I have to go now, but I'll check on you later. Be careful, Kate."

"I will." Kate switched off her phone. She remembered Johnny Castille. He'd been kind to her when a stalker moved in next door and terrorized her shortly after she'd arrived in Sage Hills.

She wandered through the house, making sure the blinds were shut in her bedroom, studio, and bathroom. Kate loved her cozy little home, especially her living room with its cream-colored walls, floral love seat, and carved cherry bookcase. The thought of it being splashed on the front page of newspapers or on television screens made her nervous. Luckily, the reporters hadn't pushed their way inside. She held her cellphone in one hand to feel a sense of security and tapped on it with the other to relieve tension. She hoped she wouldn't have to wait long for the police. Sage Hills was pretty small.

After a few tense minutes, a loud knock filled the living room. "Mrs. Stevens? Sage Hills PD."

Kate looked through the peephole and was relieved to see Johnny. "Officer Castille, I'm so glad to see you," Kate said, opening the door to find a second officer behind him. "Please come in."

She stepped aside as the officers entered the house.

"I think you know Officer Landon." Officer Castille smiled. "We wanted to make sure you were OK. Officer Landon is going to stay inside with you to get your statement while I go talk to the press. Unfortunately, there's not a whole lot I can do except make sure they stay off your property. I can't make them leave the street unless they're blocking traffic." With that, Officer Castille went back outside.

Kate let out a long sigh. "Why don't we sit down?" Kate led the way to the sitting area and sat in the Queen Anne chair as Officer Landon perched on the sofa.

Officer Landon asked Kate basic questions for the report before addressing the details of her conversation with the press. "Everyone was nonthreatening?"

"Their presence was unnerving. Nobody shouted threats, but their pushy behavior made me feel threatened." Kate sank back into the chair. "I'm not used to so much attention."

"Why all of the attention?"

Kate was sure Officer Landon was already familiar with the story, but she recounted the events at the club Saturday night and explained her connection to Cole. "I don't know how the reporters found out my name or where I lived. If Cole hadn't sung the song he wrote for me and visited my table after the show, then nobody would have known of my existence or friendship with Cole."

Officer Landon pursed his lips. "Reporters have an uncanny way of finding out these things."

Officer Castille tapped on the door and came inside. "Most of the reporters left, but there are a few diehards left on the street." He handed Kate a card. "Keep this handy. If they should return, call this number and we'll send someone back out. If anyone becomes threatening, call 911. It might be wise not to answer any phone calls from numbers you don't recognize."

Kate walked the officers to the door. "I understand. Thanks."

After they left, she collapsed on the love seat and felt very alone. She closed her eyes and took slow, deep breaths until she felt calm. A few minutes later, her eyes flew open. *Vanessa! What if she sees a broadcast with her mother and home on the screen? She'd worry.* Kate dialed Vanessa's cellphone number and was disappointed to hear her daughter's recorded voice. With as much cheer as she could muster, Kate left a quick message of caution.

As soon as she switched off the phone, it rang again and Vivi's phone number popped up on caller ID. "Vivi, I'm so glad it's you."

"I've been watching the circus from my living-room window. How are you holding up?" Vivi asked.

"I'm OK. I feel like a prisoner in my own home though. I'm calmer now that the police officers shooed away most of the press." Kate sighed. "It's been crazy."

Kate's phone beeped, indicating she had an incoming call. She pulled the phone from her ear and glanced at the number. She didn't recognize it and decided to let the call go to voice mail.

"Would you like some company? My Uncle Ray is visiting from Houston, and he'd like to meet you. I have some fresh-baked muffins to share, courtesy of Mom. I stopped by to see her yesterday, and she loaded me down with goodies."

Kate smiled for the first time since opening the door to the reporter on her doorstep. If anyone could cheer her up, it was Vivi. "That would be great, if you can get through the crowd of reporters."

"No worries. We'll see you shortly. Hang in there."

"I will. Bye." Kate put down her phone. She was relieved she'd have friendly visitors.

Kate put on the teakettle and set a small basket of assorted herbal teas on the kitchen table. She had just set out three mugs and napkins when Vivi knocked on the front door.

"Come in. Boy, am I glad to see you," Kate said, opening the door to find her friend and a stooped gentleman dressed in an oversize suit and an old-fashioned felt hat. She extended her hand to him. "Hi, I'm Kate."

When he looked up and pulled off the hat, she saw his hazel eyes and blond hair. "Cole! Are you OK?"

Without thinking, Kate gave him a hug. She stepped back and looked at him, unsure of who was more shocked at her impromptu show of affection.

Cole spoke first. "I'm sorry I didn't call last night. It was late when Evan, my lawyer, called. We talked a long time about what to expect next. You were on my mind, though."

"Why don't you two sit in here and chat while I busy myself in the kitchen?" Vivi moved the basket of muffins to her other arm. She started toward the kitchen. "The muffins will be ready when you are."

Kate watched Vivi sashay toward the now-whistling teakettle before turning to Cole. "How did you find Vivi?"

"You used one of her business cards to write the restaurant name on when we met at the club Saturday night. Her cellphone number was on it." He smiled. "You'd mentioned she lived across the street, so I called and asked for her help. It was obvious you're good friends."

"We are. She's the best." Kate walked to the sitting area. "Let's sit down."

Cole sat on the love seat. Kate opted for the chair.

"The club postponed our appearances a few days to give me time to deal with this." Cole leaned as close to the chair as the love seat arm would allow. "I haven't been arrested, but I'm their main person of interest. I'll be under close scrutiny until they find Brice's killer."

"I'm sorry, Cole." Kate scooted to the edge of her chair. "Is there anything I can do to help?"

"Not at the moment." Cole shook his head. "I just need to know you believe I didn't kill Brice. We argued, yes. But I would never kill anyone."

Kate sat back in her chair, taking time to choose her words. "We haven't seen each other in years. A lot of things can happen in that amount of time." She shook her head. "But I don't believe you'd intentionally kill anyone."

"I didn't kill him at all, Kate. He was alive when I left

him in the alley. Agitated and probably high, but alive. It's important to me that you believe that."

His eyes were intense and pleading. Kate wanted to believe him, but how could she be sure when they hadn't seen each other for so long? "I believe in you enough to help you find the real killer."

He did a few neck rolls like the ones Kate remembered from high school gym class. When he stopped, his eyes met Kate's. "What is there between you and Detective Matthews? He questioned me intensely about the murder, but he kept bringing you into the conversation. Are you two dating?"

A burning sensation traveled from Kate's neck to her cheeks. "We've been out a few times, but it's nothing serious. We met before I moved here, while I was at a needlework conference in Fort Worth." She blushed again. "I was a suspect in a murder that happened during the conference."

Cole was silent, so Kate continued. "As unbelievable as it sounds, we reconnected shortly after I moved here when I was suspected of killing my first publisher."

Just as Cole reached for Kate's hand, someone rang the doorbell and followed it with a knock on the front door. She jumped up and looked at Cole. "Maybe you'd better go into the kitchen and let me see who it is."

When Cole disappeared, Kate peeked out through the blinds. Peter stood sideways on the porch, glancing back and forth from the door to the two reporters still keeping vigil at the curb. *What is he going to think when he finds Cole here?*

"Hello, Peter," Kate said, opening the door. "Did you get pumped by the press?"

He stepped inside. "No. Both of them have covered the crime beat for years, and I know them. I just said I didn't have anything new to report."

"Off the record, do you have anything new on the case?" Kate waved him to the sofa and she returned to the chair, willing Cole to stay in the kitchen.

"Not yet. We're still checking Cole's background and trying to verify that what he said is true. And then there's the victim's background. He was hardly squeaky-clean," Peter said. "We'll get to the bottom of this. I came by to check on you."

"It was unnerving, but I'm OK." Kate glanced at the kitchen door. *Should I tell Peter that Cole is in my kitchen at this very minute?*

"Kate, I also came by to get a handle on your feelings for Cole." Peter stared into her eyes. "You two were obviously sharing a moment when I arrived at the restaurant yesterday. How well do you know him?"

"We went out several times, and he was always a gentleman." Kate smiled, remembering the day she met him at the jazz club in New York. She'd never expected a successful musician to be so kind and friendly. She thought she'd already told Peter the story. "We gradually saw less of each other because he had his career, which kept him either teaching classes or leaving on tour, and I had Vanessa and a life in Maine. We didn't have time to be serious."

A rowdy sneeze resounded from the kitchen. Peter cocked his head and looked at the kitchen door. "You have company?"

Kate cringed. This could be unpleasant. "Vivi and Cole are in the kitchen making tea. They came by to check on me too." She stood. "I'm sorry I didn't say anything. I didn't expect any company at all, and I didn't know how you'd react if you found him here."

"You're about to find out." Peter strode to the kitchen door and pushed it open. "You two may as well come out now."

Vivi and Cole emerged from the kitchen. Vivi held up

her basket with a sheepish smile. "Would you like a muffin?"

"No." Peter crossed his arms. "I'd like for you to return home and for Cole to answer a few questions."

Vivi shot a questioning look at Kate.

"It's OK, Vivi." Kate nodded. "We'll talk later. Thanks for bringing the muffins."

Vivi hugged Kate. "I'll leave them here for you. Call me."

After Vivi left the cottage, Kate returned to her chair while Peter and Cole sat on opposite sides of the love seat. Peter sat on the end next to Kate but turned to Cole. "Why are you here? You took the risk of being questioned by the media to see Kate. Why?"

"I saw the newscast with all of the reporters in front of the house. I wanted to make sure she was all right." Cole paused as if weighing what to say next. "And I needed to hear that she knows I didn't murder Brice."

Peter inhaled a large breath and let it out slowly. "I see. Her opinion is important to you." His blue eyes darkened and he arched one eyebrow. "Just what are your feelings for Kate?"

Kate shot out of her chair before Cole could answer. "Stop it, both of you!" She stood with her hands on hips. "First, there's no need to discuss me as if I'm not here. Second, Peter, this has nothing whatsoever to do with this murder. On a more personal note, I'm liking both of you less with each passing moment!"

The men sat in silence as Kate marched to the front door and turned the handle. "I want you both to leave. It's been a trying day for all of us."

Cole's eyes narrowed. "What about the reporters?"

"Put your hat on and walk right by them the way you came. They probably won't bother you. If they do, handle them however you wish; just please don't mention my name.

I have nothing to do with this investigation." She glared at Peter. "It might be nice to tell them that I'm in no way involved in the case. Maybe then I can get some peace." Kate opened the door. "Go."

After she closed the front door, Kate moved to the window and watched the two men walk to the street. Peter went directly to his car and didn't say a word to the two reporters lingering nearby. Cole crossed the road to Vivi's house, where Kate suspected the band van was parked.

Vivi emerged from her house and crossed the street. Kate let her in before she knocked and wrapped her arms around her as soon as the door was closed.

"How're you holding up?" Vivi asked.

Kate shook her head. "I'm uncomfortable with people hovering outside."

"Let's have that tea, and Mom's muffins are sitting on your kitchen table." Vivi stepped back and guided her friend toward the kitchen. "I have an idea for how we can relax for a few hours and support a good cause too."

"I'm all for anything to take my mind off the reporters outside." Kate nodded, following Vivi through the kitchen door.

They sat on opposite sides of the small rectangular table, a teapot and the basket of muffins between them. Kate filled Vivi's cup before pouring tea into her own. "Tell me about this relaxation idea of yours."

"Sage Hills Community Church still needs lap blankets for the nursing-home ministry." Vivi plucked a poppy seed muffin from the basket and plopped it onto her plate. "I know you have all sorts of extra yarn and crochet hooks around here. We can crochet away frustration and complete two blankets for the elderly by the end of the day."

"What a perfect idea." Kate sipped her tea. The dread of

avoiding reporters all day gave way to the anticipation and joy of helping others. "I have plenty of yarn in a variety of colors."

"I thought you'd like it," Vivi replied.

They finished their tea and padded down the hallway to Kate's studio to rummage through her yarn stash, select colors, and grab crochet hooks. Vivi opted for a single shade of rose, while Kate chose several pastel hues.

Less than thirty minutes later, the two friends looked like bookends sitting together on the living room love seat, their fingers quickly manipulating yarn into rows of uniform stitches. They crocheted in comfortable silence sporadically interspersed with light chitchat. Kate and Vivi worked steadily for hours, taking a quick lunch break around two o'clock before continuing their projects. No mention was made of the reporters outside or the unanswered phone calls that seemed to dwindle as the afternoon passed.

By the time Kate walked Vivi to the front door, the lap robes were completed and Kate was glad the day had passed without additional drama. "Thank you for spending the day with me. Having you here made this afternoon much easier."

"I was happy to do it." Vivi smiled, holding the two new blankets in her arms. "The nursing-home residents will be thrilled with these. Call me if you need anything tonight."

"Will do." Kate opened the door and saw her friend out.

When Vivi was safely inside her house, Kate closed the door and went to the kitchen to pour a cup of tea before returning to her favorite chair in the living room. She sat and sipped the calming herbal mixture as the silence enveloped her and the room started to darken. When her stomach reminded her she hadn't eaten much of the grilled cheese sandwich she'd fixed earlier, Kate pulled a container of chicken salad from the refrigerator. She took it to the kitchen table and ate straight from the container until it was gone. She followed that with one of Vivi's poppy seed muffins. After she finished eating and cleaning up, Kate went to the bathroom and filled the tub with warm water, added lavender oil, and washed away the unpleasantness of the day.

It was barely nine o'clock when she tied the sash on her robe and roamed through the cottage, checking to make sure the doors were locked and turning out lights. Standing in the dark, she peeked through the living room blinds. The lamppost illuminated the driveway and most of the front yard. The reporters were finally gone. She was ready for a good night's sleep. "Alone at last," she said, her voice slicing the silence.

Kate turned from the window and saw the green glow from her cellphone on the coffee table. She had been ignoring most of her phone calls throughout the day. She had messages. With little light filtering through the mini blinds, she gingerly crept toward the light blinking from her phone and sat in her chair to listen to the messages. She deleted all of the messages from the media. She listened to and saved one from Paige and another from her agent, Adam Vargas, before finding one left by the caller she'd ignored earlier in the day. Curious, she punched in the code to listen to it too.

A very thick Southern accent spilled into the air. "Mrs. Stevens, this is Jamie Martin, assistant to Texas First Lady Sophia Jackson, calling from the Governor's Mansion. Please return my call at your earliest convenience to discuss a matter of utmost importance."

Kate switched off her phone, stood up, and crossed the darkness to the light emanating from the hallway. "What a strange day."

Six

"Do you have anything to say for yourself, Mrs. Stevens?" The deep voice boomed from the darkness across the room. "I have two death warrants to sign in front of me."

Kate blinked into the light beam shining in her eyes. "No, Governor Jackson. I don't. I'm innocent."

"Then why won't you tell us the truth? Cole Cutchins killed Brice Denman, and you helped him cover it up."

The light became brighter, and Kate shielded her eyes with her left hand. "The light hurts my eyes. Please don't shine it in my face."

"Not until you explain how you helped Cutchins kill Denman." The voice was as unnerving as the light.

"No. I'm innocent." *Why won't he listen?* "I don't know who killed Mr. Denman. I didn't even know him."

A loud *bang* echoed through the room from a chair that was knocked over by someone quickly standing up. The light kept her from seeing who it was.

"You're a liar." Peter's voice assaulted her ears. "I found you conspiring with the suspect. Plotting his escape."

"Peter! No!"

Kate sat up to find sunlight filtering through the slats of the mini blinds in her bedroom. Her heart was thundering in her chest as her gaze swept the room. Her grandmother's blue glass perfume bottle was still nestled on its crocheted doily on the dresser between Vanessa's high school graduation photo and a carved wood jewelry box, a gift from her mother years ago. Everything was as it should be. She eased her head back onto the plump pillow, closed her eyes, and took several deep breaths. "Just a dream. A weird dream."

Her eyes flew open when she remembered the message from the Governor's Mansion. *Was that a dream too?* Rolling toward the antique maple nightstand, Kate reached out and grabbed her cellphone before settling back on the pillow to listen to her messages. Sure enough, a representative from the Governor's Mansion had called. But why? She *had* been in the press a lot over the last few days, but would that warrant such a call?

Kate checked the time on her cellphone. It was just after eight o'clock. She tried to remember if Vivi had mentioned what time she needed to be at work this morning. Her hours changed according to what events were planned each week. Would Vivi have time to chat? Kate needed to talk about this phone call before she made it. She sent her friend a quick text message, jumped out of bed, and changed into shorts and T-shirt. By the time she'd dressed, Vivi had replied. "Come on over. Coffee's made. No reporters outside."

"The Governor's Mansion?" The coffee Vivi was pouring for Kate nearly missed the mug. "Any idea why they'd be calling you?"

"No, unless it has something to do with the murder and Cole being a suspect. I don't understand, but I've been all over the media the last few days. People want to make our relationship into something it isn't." Kate took the steaming mug from Vivi's hands. "I usually keep a low profile. I'm not one to be attracting the attention of the rich and powerful."

Vivi poured another cup of coffee and sat across the kitchen table from Kate. "I guess there's only one way to find out." She blew the steam curling above the cup. "Call."

"You're right." Kate frowned. "But I'd feel better if I knew the topic before I called. And what's an appropriate time to return a call to the Governor's Mansion?"

"Nine o'clock would be good. If it's too early or they're busy, leave a message and they'll call back," Vivi said, turning to peer at the clock on the microwave. "I have a meeting at ten o'clock, but I still have time to stay while you call. I can't stay long after because I'll need to set up my presentation. We're trying to land a three-day medical conference, so I need to be at my best."

"Which explains the linen suit when it's going to be around a hundred degrees today." Kate sipped her coffee. "Sounds important."

"It is," Vivi said. "But not quite so important as being summoned by an assistant to the first lady of Texas. I hope you get through on the first try. I sure would like to know what's up before I go to the meeting."

"I'll call Jamie Martin right at nine o'clock." Kate drummed her fingers on her mug.

Vivi looked at the clock. "We'll know soon." She stood up and put her mug in the sink. "Finish your coffee and feel free to have a refill while I get my things together."

"Thanks for sticking around for the call." Kate smiled. "I appreciate the backup."

"Anytime. It'll just take me a few minutes to get ready," Vivi said, disappearing through the dining room to the hallway.

Leaning back into the white French country chair, Kate took a deep breath to calm her nerves. Sitting in Vivi's cheery, neat kitchen always brightened her mood. The white glass-front cabinets showed neat stacks of plain white dishes and a few cobalt blue accent pieces. Several small pots of herbs lined the windowsill. Like its owner, this was an efficient, friendly kitchen. Kate was blessed to have found a dear friend so soon after moving to Sage Hills.

Kate drained the coffee from her mug and took it to the sink, where she rinsed it and the one Vivi had used. She practiced the words she'd say when her call to the Governor's Mansion was answered. Ms. Martin likely wouldn't be answering the phone. "Hello, my name is Kate Stevens. I'm returning a call to Jamie Martin." She repeated it, changing the wording several different ways. She liked the first version best; it was short and to the point.

"Your spiel sounds good." Vivi's shoes clicked on the light tile floor. "It's almost nine. Are you ready?"

"Yes, I'm ready." Kate picked up her cellphone and dialed as Vivi gave her the thumbs-up.

She drew in a deep breath and let it out slowly as the phone rang. She jumped when a vaguely familiar voice answered. "First Lady Sophia Jackson's office, Jamie Martin speaking. How may I help you?"

Kate's speech spilled out in one nervous breath. Her heart rate slowed as Vivi briefly laid a hand on her shoulder before sitting in the chair across from her.

"Mrs. Stevens, thank you for returning my call." Jamie Martin's voice reminded Kate of magnolia blossoms and mint juleps. "You may remember me as Jamielyn Martinez. We met last week at Once Upon a Yarn in Fort Worth. We discussed crochet wedding dresses."

"Yes, I remember." It'd been less than a week since they'd met in Paige's shop, but a lot had happened since then. "How's the wedding dress search?"

"Actually, we've reached a decision," Ms. Martin said. "After looking at countless designers and researching your background, Governor Jackson's daughter, Carolina, has chosen you to design and create a wedding dress especially for her. Would you be available to meet with Miss Jackson and her mother tomorrow morning?"

"Governor Jackson's daughter wants me to design her wedding dress? I'm honored, Ms. Martin. Tomorrow morning?" Kate's mind was spinning. She nearly chuckled when she looked up and saw Vivi's head bobbing up and down with enthusiasm.

"Yes," Kate said, "I can meet with you tomorrow."

"I realize this is short notice, but the first lady had a cancellation, and Miss Carolina is most anxious to get started on her dress. Is ten o'clock convenient for you?"

"Yes, ten o'clock is fine." Kate paused. "May I bring an assistant with me? Her name is Vivi Lawrence."

"Excellent. Miss Jackson will be pleased. Yes, please bring your assistant. I'll email a confirmation and instructions to the address on your card. We'll see you tomorrow."

"I look forward to it. Thank you so much." Kate switched off her phone and looked at Vivi with wide eyes. "You want to go to the Governor's Mansion tomorrow?"

Vivi jumped up and gave her a bear hug. "Woo-hoo! You're designing a wedding dress for the daughter of our governor!" Vivi released her. "Luckily, I'm working tomorrow night, so I'm free to be your assistant during the day."

"Thanks for going with me. I think I'd be too nervous to go alone. I hope I can get some design work done this morning. Paige is waiting for me to fill an empty mannequin. I'd like to have a sheer, white, floral-lace shirt finished for her in the next week."

"If this meeting goes my way, I might be getting off early today. Would you like to go check out the new bookstore that opened on Main Street?" Vivi said, shrugging into the linen jacket she'd hung on the back of a kitchen chair. "It might help get your mind off the Cole situation."

Kate walked to the front door. "A trip to the bookstore will be a nice incentive for me to get my work done. Call me after your meeting."

"Will do." Vivi grabbed her briefcase and purse.

They left through the front door, Vivi heading to her car and Kate trotting across the street. Kate was almost to her front steps when a royal blue compact car pulled to the curb, its horn beeping twice. She was surprised to see Cole emerge from the driver's side.

"Kate! I'm glad you're here," he called, stepping onto the curb.

She turned and met him in the middle of the sidewalk. "Hi, Cole. Nice ride. What happened to the van?"

"The PD still has it. I didn't want to cool my heels in the hotel room, so I rented a car." He took a step forward. "I found Brice's parents online. They still live in Sage Hills. Will you visit them with me?"

"I'm not so sure this is a good idea. Did you run the idea by your attorney?" Kate asked.

"I mentioned it," Cole said, shaking his head. "Evan wasn't too keen on the idea. He said it wouldn't look good for me to contact the victim's parents before I've been cleared. But talking to them might lead to another suspect."

"It might not go over too well with the police, either." Kate wanted to help Cole, but she didn't want to risk digging him deeper into trouble. "Do you really think the Denmans will talk to you?"

"Maybe. I met them years ago when I was an adjunct professor at the University of Texas and played in a local band with Brice. They came to our gigs a lot." He looked down and scuffed the concrete. "I've got to do something. It's worth a try, isn't it?"

"Maybe." Kate stepped onto the porch. "Have you tried to call them?"

Cole nodded. "Twice. After I went back to the hotel last night and again this morning. I got their voice mail both times and left messages asking if they'd talk to me."

Kate saw determination in those hazel eyes. "Then you're right; the next thing to do is to go see them."

"Will you go with me?" His voice was pleading. "They might be more willing to talk if I'm not alone. Your friend Peter doesn't seem too anxious to clear me. I need to do this."

Kate turned to her door and unlocked it. Should she go? She didn't agree with Peter's take on Cole, but she'd feel better if Vivi could go with them. After all, Cole was a murder suspect. Accompanying him would push her deeper into the murder investigation. Still, at one time, they'd meant a lot to each other. That should mean something.

"Come on in. I can't go to the Denmans' in shorts and flip-flops." Kate stepped inside and held the door open for Cole.

"OK, but you look fine," he said, stepping into the living room.

Cole checked the car's GPS. "I hope the Denmans will remember the good times when Brice and I were friends, before the drugs."

The neighborhoods changed from older clapboard cottage-style houses to large Victorian showplaces to simple ranch-style homes popular in the early 1970s. The GPS led them to a small, ungated subdivision of well-maintained but plain homes called Magnolia Heights. Douglas and Helen Denman lived in a yellow-and-white home that was immaculate, with bright fuchsia azalea bushes lining the front of the house and a large magnolia tree in the center of the front yard.

Cole pulled the car as close to the curb as possible, cut the engine, and sighed. "Ready?"

"As ready as you are."

They took the short walkway to the house in silence. Kate hung back as Cole stepped forward to ring the doorbell. The memory of reporters showing up unannounced was still fresh in her mind. A wreath created with ribbons and mini balls of yarn in brilliant colors greeted them with "Welcome to Our Home." Kate couldn't imagine how difficult seeing Cole would be for Brice Denman's parents. *Just how welcome will we be?*

The door opened, shaking the wreath's ribbons. "Cole Cutchins. You have a lot of nerve coming here." Douglas Denman was thin and slightly stooped; his gray hair was unkempt, and he looked as if he had missed a lot of sleep recently.

"Mr. Denman, I'm so sorry about Brice. Please, I need to speak with you." Cole motioned Kate closer. "This is my friend, Kate Stevens."

Kate nodded. "I'm so sorry for your loss."

"You'll be even sorrier if you stay where you're not wanted. Now get off my property." His words were sharp but his eyes were brimming with tears. He slammed the door.

Unmoving, Cole stared at the door.

"Let's go, Cole." Kate gently tugged his arm. "They're hurting."

"I know," Cole said, letting Kate lead him down the walkway.

Just as they reached the driveway, the door opened again. "Cole. Wait." A petite woman with chin-length gray hair and tear-stained cheeks walked toward them. "Forgive my husband. Won't you please come in? I'd like to talk to you."

Helen Denman ushered Kate and Cole into the living room and waved a hand at the sofa. "Please sit down." Mr. Denman stood stoically off to the side, barely acknowledging their presence.

Kate's gaze went straight to an eye-catching afghan with a pyramid pattern of pastel colors. "Your afghan is gorgeous. Did you make it, Mrs. Denman?"

"Yes, I did. Do you—" Her eyes flew open. "Doug said your name is Kate Stevens. Are you the Kate Stevens who writes the column in *Hook and Needle Arts*?"

Kate smiled, and the familiar flush flooded her cheeks. "Yes, I am."

"I read your column in every issue! I love your work."

"Thank you." Kate noticed crocheted doilies on each table in the room as well as a large framed piece just inside the front door. "Your work is beautiful. And thank you for seeing us. Cole has been concerned about you."

"It's been the most difficult thing we've ever experienced." Helen Denman's eyes again filled with tears. "Cole, you knew Brice when he was still himself—easygoing, talented, thoughtful. He was never the same after he was kicked out of the band in New York. He was filled with hatred, for you and for himself. We knew he was using drugs, but it was like that was the last straw. When he returned home, we hardly knew him. What happened up there?"

Kate and the Denmans listened as Cole told the tale of

Brice's descent into cocaine addiction, his explosive arguments with bandmates, and missed gigs. "We tried to get him help. He'd be OK for a while, but then he'd relapse. Each relapse was worse than the last. Finally, we had no choice but to let him go."

Cole stopped talking and a thick silence settled over the room. A dog began barking from the back of the house, and Mr. Denman rose and disappeared down the hallway. The barking stopped.

"I didn't realize it went back so far. It certainly explains why we didn't hear from him while he was in New York," Mrs. Denman finally said. "He hid it from us until he came back to Texas and told us he'd been kicked out of the band. We thought losing the band pushed him into drug abuse. We didn't know you'd tried to help him."

Cole leaned toward Brice's mother. "Mrs. Denman, I didn't kill Brice. It's important you believe me. I may have failed him as a friend, and I'll always regret that, but I never wished him harm."

The older woman's lip quivered. "The police detective said Brice disrupted your performance on Saturday and the two of you quarreled afterward. What was it about?"

"He accused me of ruining his life when I kicked him out of the band." Cole's voice caught as Douglas Denman returned to his chair. He glanced at the grieving father before continuing. "It hurt me to do it. We'd played in bands together for more than a decade. He was so talented when he was straight." A tear slid down Cole's cheek. "On Saturday, I offered to help him. Brice wouldn't listen to me. Instead, he pulled out a gun. But I swear to you, he was alive when I walked out of that alley."

"I believe you, Cole." Mrs. Denman reached for his hand and held it for a moment. "I remember when you two were as close as brothers." Her voice broke. "He battled addiction for a long time, and he was feeling more positive about his music. He'd started writing songs, recording them, and posting them online. He was encouraged by comments posted by listeners. I really thought he was going to straighten out his life with these new songs. They gave him hope."

Neither the Denmans nor Cole seemed able to continue. Kate coughed softly. "Mr. Denman, Mrs. Denman, do you have any idea who might have done this?"

Brice's parents exchanged a look. Mr. Denman spoke for the first time since they had come into the house. "His girlfriend recently broke up with him," he said. "She dumped all of his belongings on the sidewalk outside his apartment building and told him he could die for all she cared. Brice was crushed."

"He was already reeling from the breakup," Mrs. Denman added. "When you showed up on tour—well, I guess it made him snap." Mrs. Denman looked Cole in the eye. "I suggest you talk to her, Gwen Wright. She lives in Fort Worth. I think the apartments are called the Garden Terrace. Garden something. She drives an ancient Toyota Corolla. Blue."

Mr. Denman shifted in his chair. "Be careful. Gwen has an explosive temper."

"We'll be careful," Cole said, standing. "Thank you."

Mr. and Mrs. Denman rose and stood side by side.

"Thank *you* for seeking the truth." Mrs. Denman grabbed Cole's hand and held it between hers. "Please keep us posted on what you find."

"We will." Cole stepped toward the door and Kate followed.

"I'm sorry we met under these circumstances," Kate said. "But I'm glad we met."

The front door didn't close until Kate and Cole reached the car.

Seven

Kate and Cole were sitting at her kitchen table, eating sandwiches and looking up information about Gwen Wright on the laptop, when Vivi called.

"Are you ready to hit the bookstore?" Vivi sounded jubilant. "We can celebrate my new account with a new addition to my bookshelf."

"Congratulations!" Kate pushed the print icon to make a copy of a newspaper listing of arrests including one Gwen Wright for aggravated assault. "I know you're looking forward to exploring the bookstore, but how would you like to play private investigator instead?"

"You have my attention. What's up?"

Kate gave her an abbreviated account of the visit with the Denmans. "We've been searching for information about Gwen Wright for an hour or so. We found the address of her apartment building and an arrest affidavit for assault from four years ago." Kate walked to her studio and snagged the affidavit from the printer. "It looks like she was jealous of a woman who was giving her boyfriend at the time a little too much attention."

Vivi whistled. "You think she might have killed Denman?"

"Maybe. His parents seem to think it's a possibility." Kate entered the kitchen and handed the arrest affidavit to Cole while continuing her conversation with Vivi. "Would you like to go with us to talk to her? We could use someone more familiar with Fort Worth than either of us."

"I'd love it. I'm about fifteen minutes from home. Give me a few extra minutes to change into cooler clothes and I'll be right there."

"Sounds great. We'll see you soon."

"You did *what*?" Peter's voice was laced with disapproval. Kate was relieved this conversation was taking place over the phone. "And they let you in?"

"Yes, because Cole knew the Denmans from when he taught music in Austin years ago and played in a band with Brice." Knowing she sounded defensive, Kate took a deep breath. Irritating Peter wouldn't help Cole's case. "They were tentative at first, but deep down they knew Brice had been into drugs a long time."

"They didn't mention an ex-girlfriend to me."

"Maybe they did, but you didn't want to hear it because you're so intent on hanging this on Cole." Kate clapped her hand over her mouth, unable to believe she'd said the thought aloud. Cole, sitting beside her in the driver's seat of his rental car, smiled. Kate refocused. "Her name is Gwen Wright and she lives in Fort Worth."

"Can you give me specifics, at least an area of the city?" Peter ignored her dig.

"Not really, no." Kate bit her lip at her half-truth. She really couldn't because then he might possibly reach Gwen Wright's place before she, Cole, and Vivi had a chance to talk with her. "I just wanted to let you know about the girlfriend. She might be important."

"Thanks. I'll look into it."

"I'm happy to help. I need to get back to work now." She watched Cole turn the steering wheel and ease the car onto the interstate.

"Wait, what can you tell me about the Denmans?" Peter interjected before Kate had a chance to sign off. "Anything I should know?"

Kate described the demeanor of Brice's parents and how they gradually opened up more about their son. When she realized she'd begun repeating herself, it was time to end the call. "Peter, I really need to go. Call me later, OK?"

"OK. And Kate, don't talk to anyone else about the investigation—and by all means, don't spend so much time with Cole."

"Just trust me, Peter. And take care out there." Kate sighed and switched off her phone. "That was awkward."

"I didn't think he would ever let you off the phone," Vivi said, leaning forward and putting her hand on the back of Kate's seat. "Think he was trying to trip you up?"

"Maybe." Kate glanced into the backseat. "You never know. Cops can be sly like that."

"Especially when the cop is jealous of the primary suspect," Cole said. "How far are we from Gwen Wright's place anyway? The GPS seems confused."

"They've added a couple new exits on this stretch of highway, so that may be why. Take the next exit and head south." Still leaning forward, Vivi pointed to a large sign with distances to the next three exits. "It'll be several blocks before you turn again. Kate, the apartment isn't too far from where we met Vanessa for lunch, but in some ways, they're worlds apart."

Kate turned her head from side to side as the car glided off the interstate and into an area of littered streets and graffiti-marked buildings. "It always amazes me to see how the personality of a city can change from one neighborhood to the next."

The neighborhood improved slightly when Cole turned onto Prosperity Street, but the buildings were still dingy and rundown. "Interesting example of prosperity." Cole looked at the GPS. "Technology caught up with us. Looks like the Garden Terrace Apartments are just ahead."

Gwen Wright's U-shaped apartment building looked like a 1970s concrete-block hotel converted into apartments. Heavy drapes were closed in every apartment, as if each unit had shut its eyes in pain. The mustard yellow color with brown trim looked hideous, but Kate gave the owners brownie points for applying what looked like a fresh coat of paint. A line of thirsty boxwood plants lined the parking lot. "I wonder where the mailboxes are."

"Don't know, but I see an old blue Corolla in the right corner space." Cole pulled into one of several empty parking spaces along the front of the building. "The parking spaces are numbered; maybe they correspond with the units."

Kate ran her eyes along the numbers on the curb. "If so, and if that is her car, then Gwen lives in 210."

"What are the odds of someone else in this place having a twenty-year-old blue Corolla?" Vivi unbuckled her seat belt and slid to the driver's side of the car. "There are some unmarked spaces at the other end from the Corolla. Maybe we should park there. This might be someone's assigned spot. We don't want to attract any attention."

"True." Cole backed the car out and maneuvered it into an unmarked space. "Here we go."

Kate mopped the perspiration from her face with a tissue as she closed the car door. "They need to plant some shade trees."

"You're lucky to get the boxwoods." Vivi led the way across the parking lot. "Not much grows here in the summer unless it's watered regularly. It's not likely this place has a working irrigation system."

They found a set of concrete stairs between the back and right side of the horseshoe. Gwen Wright's apartment was to the right as they emerged onto the second floor. Cole reached up to knock on the door, but Kate grabbed his arm before his fist could connect with it. "A woman knocking might seem less threatening."

Cole stepped aside, giving Kate room to reach the door. She rapped three times and studied the pattern of the dried paint on the wood while she prayed the Denmans were exaggerating the severity of Gwen Wright's temper.

The door opened a few inches, allowing a peek at an eye and frizzy dark blond hair of the tenant. "Yes?"

"Hello. I'm Kate Stevens. I'm looking for Gwen Wright."

The eye didn't blink. "Why?"

"I, or *we*," Kate said, gesturing to Vivi and Cole, "want to talk to her about Brice Denman."

The door remained cracked, but the eye disappeared. Soon more of the face appeared in the window, where a hand held the drapes back a few inches. The drape fell, and the chain soon rattled. "I'm Gwen." The door opened wider. "Who are you? You don't look like cops."

Cole moved closer to the door. "I'm Cole Cutchins. I was in a band with Brice a long time ago."

"They say you killed him." The words rode on a velvety Southern accent. She sounded tired.

"I didn't kill him." Cole leaned forward. "But I'm trying to find out who did."

Vivi put her hand on Cole's arm and moved him aside.

"Gwen, I'm Vivi. Kate and I are helping Cole find out the truth about Brice's death. Could we please talk to you a few minutes? We won't keep you long."

The door opened wider and Gwen stepped aside to allow them into the apartment. The furniture was worn, as was the threadbare beige carpet, but it was of good quality. Kate's eyes were immediately pulled to the impressionistic painting of an urban skyline hanging over the sofa. "What a stunning painting." Kate moved to the center of the room. "The reds look perfect with the sofa."

"Thank you." Gwen motioned them to the sofa as she sank into a dark blue leather chair, also well used. "The painting is the reason I kicked Brice out of the apartment and my life."

Kate sat on the end of the sofa closest to Gwen, whose blue eyes and thick, wavy hair reminded her of the actress Sarah Jessica Parker. "You're welcome. The painting is the reason you kicked Brice out of the apartment?" Kate crossed her legs and rested her hands on her knees. "Why?"

Gwen gazed at the painting for several seconds. "The painting belonged to my grandmother. When I was a little girl, I would stare at it and dream I lived in that colorful city where I imagined everybody was happy. Grandma said I had to make wherever I lived my happy city. It was one of the few things she owned of any value. I inherited it when she died."

She bowed her head for a moment before looking up to Kate again. "I'm working two jobs to save money to go to college. I want to study computer programming, get a good job, and move to a better place. My days are spent as a billing clerk for a pharmaceutical company. At night I clean offices. I'm gone a lot. You found me home today because I've been a mess since Brice was killed, so I took some sick time to get my head back on straight." Gwen took a deep breath and rubbed her temples. "I came home one day to change clothes before going to my night job and the painting was gone. Brice had pawned it for drug money. It was more than I could handle. I exploded and threw everything of his over the balcony."

Vivi cleared her throat. "When was that?"

"A couple of months ago. He tried to contact me on and off until he—died." Tears started flowing. "I'm so sorry I handled things so badly."

"Gwen, you did the best you could. Trust me, I've been there." Images of Harry's drunken rampages during their marriage flashed through Kate's mind. "Sometimes you just have to walk away."

The crying stopped. "I know, but I wish I'd handled it better."

"Sometimes we handle it without thinking. It's survival." Kate chanced a very small smile. "You will survive. You'll make it to your happy city."

"I know." Gwen mirrored Kate's smile.

"Tell us about Brice," Cole said.

Gwen's eyes moved to Cole. "You said Brice was your friend, so you know the roller coaster he was always on. When he was sober, he was the sweetest guy on the planet, but drugs and alcohol turned him into a monster." She pulled a tissue from the box on the coffee table. "I tried so hard to help him, but it was too much for me to handle. You understand, don't you?"

Cole nodded. "I'd hoped he'd get help when he lost his gig with my band, but it sounds like he only got worse. I'm sorry."

"The newspaper said Brice jumped you in the alley behind the jazz club. That true?"

"Yes."

She wiped her tears, leaving a streak of eyeliner on her cheek. "He had a gun?"

"He did, yes."

"Reporters don't seem to believe you about Brice having the gun." Gwen brushed a piece of lint from the chair and raised her eyes to Cole. "I believe you." Her voice was barely audible. "He pulled one on me too."

A gurgling sound came from the kitchen, followed by a louder rumble as the icemaker dumped ice into the freezer. At a loss for words, Kate waited for Gwen to continue. Cole and Vivi were also silent.

Gwen wiped her nose. "His failure as a musician pushed him over the edge, and I just couldn't pull him back. I loved him, but when he was using, he got violent. One time he was so high that I'm not sure he could tell what was reality, and he pulled a gun on me. I was terrified. Finally, I got to the point where I couldn't take it anymore. The painting was the last straw."

That could be a motive for murder. Mr. Denman's warning echoed in Kate's mind. *"Watch out, she has an explosive temper."* But Gwen didn't seem too volatile to Kate.

Cole leaned forward. "Do you know where we can find any of Brice's friends?"

"He'd alienated most of his friends, but there was a guy at the music store in Dallas who would get him gigs and encouraged him to make music videos and post them online. His name is Dexter Young. The store was called Good Time Music, but it changed recently. I don't remember the new name. Dexter might be able to help you."

Kate was sure Gwen wasn't the killer, but she wanted proof. "Gwen, where were you Saturday night?"

Gwen's dark eyes widened. "You think I killed him?"

"No, I don't. I just want to make sure we've covered everything before we move on to someone else."

"I was at my friend's bachelorette party in Dallas. I didn't get home until after one in the morning."

Vivi stood up. "Do you mind if I use your restroom?"

Gwen pointed down the hallway. "Second door on the left. The first is a linen closet."

Kate watched Vivi disappear down the hallway before she spoke again. "Do you mind telling us the name of your friend who's getting married?"

"Why do you need her name?"

"We're just trying to gather as much information as possible so we can clear Cole," Kate answered.

Gwen rubbed her eyes. "Her name is Angel Lauria. Please don't involve her in this. She just had a party."

"We won't," Cole said. "The name of the bar?"

"Heartbeat." Gwen half smiled at Cole's amused reaction. "Seriously. What better place for a bachelorette party?"

Kate looked up just in time to see Vivi standing at the end of the hallway and holding up her phone to get a photo, presumably of Gwen. As soon as the phone was safely in Vivi's pocket, Kate stood. "You've been very helpful. We appreciate your time."

"I'm glad I could help more." Gwen stood and led the way to the door. "The Denmans really hate me, don't they?"

Cole shook his head. "I've known them a long time. They don't hate anyone. They feel guilty and sad, just like you." Gwen's eyes welled with tears again, and Cole placed his hand on her shoulder. "I want to find out who killed Brice, but not just to clear my name. I want bring closure to all of us."

Eight

Kate was standing in her bathrobe, staring into her closet, when Vivi rang the doorbell the next morning. What did one wear to a command performance at the Governor's Mansion? She tightened the belt on her robe and padded down the hallway to answer the door.

"You're not dressed!" Vivi swept into the living room. "Why?"

Kate bit her lip. "I can't decide what to wear."

"I vote for the two-piece lavender set, the one you made to wear to the publisher's party in May. It'll show off your amazing crochet skills, plus you look fab in that color."

Kate led Vivi back to the closet. She pulled out the lavender combo and held it up, one piece in each hand. "Yes, I think you're right."

"Of course I am," said Vivi, her head buried in the bottom of the closet. A few seconds later, she held up a pair of beige strappy sandals. "Wear these shoes. Do you have any jewelry, a strand of pearls maybe?"

"I do." Kate smiled, remembering the going-away party the Hook and Needle Club had given her just before she left Stony Point. They'd taken a collection and presented her with the most beautiful string of pearls she'd ever seen. They'd said she'd need a classy piece of jewelry to wear for television and magazine interviews. So far, she'd only worn them for the publicity photo on her website and to a couple of events sponsored by her publisher. She crossed the room, lifted the lid of her jewelry box, and held the pearls up for Vivi to see. "What do you think?"

"Perfect. Just the right length to fill the V-neck of the top." Vivi checked her watch. "You have five minutes before we need to hit the road."

"At least I have my makeup done already." Kate laid the pearls on her dresser. "I won't need five minutes."

"Wow," was all Kate could say when they approached the Texas Governor's Mansion on Colorado Street. She'd been in beautiful homes before, but the stately Greek revival mansion with its Ionic columns across the front took her breath away.

Vivi chuckled. "Did I thank you for inviting me along on this trip? I've always wanted to see the inside of the Governor's Mansion. Today I also get to meet the first lady and her daughter. I feel so privileged."

"Are you kidding?" Kate shot Vivi a comical look. "I'd be a bundle of nerves if I had driven the three hours to Austin alone. I'm glad you're with me."

Kate pulled the van around to the Capitol visitors' parking garage Jamie Martin had indicated on the map she'd emailed the day before. She tried to slow her breathing. *I'm meeting the governor's wife and daughter!* Where else would her new life in Texas take her?

Kate and Vivi strolled up the walkway and stopped at the top of the steps. Kate's eyes drifted from the base of one imposing column up to the scrollwork on top. She loved the strong lines and simple but elegant design. "I can't believe we're here."

They went through the main entrance and waited for Ms. Martin, who would escort them to see the first lady and her daughter. Kate clutched her portfolio in both hands as she strolled around the lobby. "I hope she likes my designs enough to retain me."

"I expect she already likes your work or you wouldn't have gotten that phone call." Vivi grinned. "I don't think you have anything to worry about."

"Then why am I so nervous?"

"It's survival instinct coupled with fear of the unknown." Vivi squeezed Kate's elbow. "You'll be fine once you meet the bride-to-be and her mother and realize they're normal people just like us. Besides, you *are* a talented designer. Have faith in yourself. Concentrate on how exciting it is to be a part of this wedding."

Before Kate could answer, she heard her name spoken behind her. "Kate Stevens?" Kate turned to see the wedding planner they'd met in Once Upon a Yarn. "Thank you for coming."

Jamie Martin smiled. "I'm sorry about the small ruse at the shop last week. When I'm out on private business for the Jacksons, I use the name Jamielyn Martinez to get around unnoticed. Please call me Jamie."

They followed Jamie to the small parlor, a light-filled, yellow room featuring a crystal chandelier, ceiling-to-floor draped curtains, and a portrait of historical icon Sam Houston, his countenance presiding over activities from above the white mantle.

Mother and daughter were standing in front of a huge window, the sunlight creating a soft halo around their heads. They turned around at the sound of Jamie's voice. "First Lady Sophia Jackson and Miss Carolina Jackson, may I present designer Kate Stevens and her assistant, Vivi Lawrence."

The first lady, who was several inches shorter than Kate despite her high heels, held out her hand. "Welcome to Austin. It's a pleasure to meet you."

Kate grasped the offered hand and smiled, focusing on giving a firm, confident handshake. "Likewise. Thank you."

"And this is my daughter, Carolina." The first lady presented her daughter with the sweep of her left hand.

Carolina tossed her head and sent her highlighted brown hair cascading down her back before holding out her hand. "Thank you for coming on such short notice." She shot an almost imperceptible glare at her mother. "I'm anxious to see your designs."

"It's an honor to be invited to share in your wedding, Miss Jackson," Kate said, shaking Carolina's hand.

Introductions completed, Jamie ushered Kate to the wood-trimmed sofa where she was joined by the first lady and Carolina. Jamie and Vivi sat in two matching antique chairs across from them.

"I see you've brought your portfolio," Carolina said.

"I did." Kate's leather case rested on her knees. "I've designed a number of formal gowns. I'd like to see which styles you like best." She nodded to a folder nestled between two candlesticks on the coffee table. "Do you have pictures of dresses for me to see?" Kate waited until she saw Carolina's nod before continuing. "That's good. They'll help me pinpoint exactly what you want for your wedding dress. Let's look through those first."

Kate flipped through the folder of pictures with Carolina and her mother. By the time they turned the last page, Kate knew she was in for a challenge. The bride and her mother wanted two totally different styles. One preferred sleek and plunging, and the other, Southern belle ruffles. The daughter was daring and contemporary. Her mother was traditional and liked lots of lace.

"Carolina, I don't know why you refuse to have your dress made by my dear friend Marisa Sanchez." Sophia Jackson turned to Kate. "Marisa is dressing all of the political elite these days, and she's right here in Austin."

"*Mother.*" Carolina pursed her lips. "It's *my* wedding, and I want a crocheted dress made by the designer of my choice. And I choose Kate."

Sophia Jackson stood up. "That's enough, Carolina."

But it wasn't enough for her daughter. Carolina turned her head to Kate. "Please don't take offense, and please excuse my mother. I definitely want you to design my wedding dress."

Kate nodded then shot an incredulous stare at Vivi, who sat silently gripping the chair arms. *How does one respond in this type of situation?* Kate started with a deep breath. "I'm familiar with Marisa Sanchez Designs. They're lovely." Kate returned the folder of pictures to the coffee table and opened her portfolio. "Let me show you my wedding dress designs. I can combine your favorite ideas from your photos and my portfolio to design the perfect dress for you."

Carolina was far more emotive over Kate's designs than those in the folder. "I love this mermaid-style gown with the plunging neckline and back." She traced the dress with her index finger. "But it's an outdoor wedding, and I'd burn up in long sleeves."

A smile tugged at Kate's lips. The dress was one of her favorites too. "I can easily re-design this as a sleeveless dress. I can add an empire waist if you like."

"I love it." Carolina's eyes glowed. "Will you be able to have sketches next week?"

After setting an appointment for the following week, when

Kate would have several designs for Carolina and her mother to consider, Jamie escorted Kate and Vivi to the entry foyer and promised an email confirmation of the next meeting. Then she disappeared.

Kate blew out a sigh of relief as she and Vivi passed between two huge columns and down the steps to the front walk. "I had my doubts there for a few minutes."

"You handled it splendidly." Vivi put an arm around her friend. "To celebrate, I'll treat you to lunch at The Driskill."

Kate stopped in her tracks across the street from The Driskill Hotel and stared at the grande dame of Austin hospitality. The breeze that had made the six-block walk from the mansion to the hotel bearable in the summer heat gently waved the American and Texas flags over the columned, arched entrance. "I understand why you wanted to have lunch here." Her eyes roamed from the steer head perched over the hotel's name to the three arches below it, down the stately columns to the main entrance. "I can feel the history already."

Vivi linked her arm through Kate's and led her off the curb. "Wait until you see the inside, not to mention taste the food."

Cloaked in opulent hues of deep red and gold, The Driskill Grill was one of the most gorgeous restaurants Kate had ever seen. She followed the hostess over the star-studded carpet through a maze of gold-clad tables, each with a bud vase of fresh flowers and a candle. This was the perfect way to cap their visit to the Governor's Mansion.

Kate and Vivi perused the menu, each opting to try one

of the creative salads on the menu—blackened shrimp and spinach for Kate, cantaloupe and crab for Vivi. Their conversation drifted from their shock at the first lady bringing up another designer and the friction between mother and daughter to Vivi's experiences with not-so-blushing brides and domineering moms. Kate was thankful to escape the topics of Cole and murder for a while. She let herself be absorbed in the historical electricity of the hotel. They received their salads and had fallen into a companionable silence when two well-heeled young women and presumably their mothers were seated at the next table. The young redhead held a phone to one ear and every few seconds would gasp, "You don't say."

Kate rolled her eyes. "I don't understand why young people can't enter a restaurant without a phone glued to an ear."

"Me either." Vivi glanced over her shoulder to see the culprit. "I wonder why her mom doesn't say something."

"Beats me." Kate speared a bite of shrimp and spinach on her fork and dipped it into the dressing cup.

It stopped halfway to her mouth when Cellphone Girl gasped and nearly shouted, "Your mother actually mentioned Marisa Sanchez in front of your designer?"

Kate's fork clattered to her plate, the shrimp and spinach stuck to its prongs. Vivi's head turned sharply. They were now eavesdropping.

"How were you supposed to know your mom promised Marisa Sanchez the dress?" The redheaded friend of Carolina Jackson paused. "No, you're right. It's *your* wedding. What did the designer do?" Another pause. "Very classy. I love it. Look, I gotta go. Mom's giving me the evil eye."

As the girl said goodbye, Vivi motioned Kate to lean closer. "That sure explains a lot."

"I guess I'll forgive the cellphone rudeness this time. I

just hope Vanessa knows better." Kate took the bite of salad waiting on her fork.

They finished their meal, paid the check, and took a quick look around the hotel before walking back to Kate's van in the Capitol parking garage. Kate started the engine, turned on the air conditioner, and pulled her cellphone from her purse. "I have two missed calls from Peter and a message from Cole."

"You're a popular lady," Vivi said. "A man for each arm."

"Oh, please." Kate dialed her voice mail and listened to Cole's velvety voice ask if she was free for dinner. She deleted the message and looked at Vivi. "Cole invited me to dinner tonight, but to be honest with you, I don't know if I want to go out this evening. Life has been so weird since Cole showed up."

"We have a three-hour drive home. Why don't you think about it awhile and then decide?" Vivi buckled her seat belt. "You might change your mind."

Kate was about to slide her cellphone into her purse when it rang. "It's Peter again."

"You may as well answer it or he'll keep calling," Vivi said.

"You're right." Kate swiped the screen to accept the call. "Hello, Peter."

"Where have you been? I've been trying to reach you all morning." His Southern drawl was laced with equal parts concern and irritation.

"I had an appointment in Austin. I'm on my way back home now." Kate glanced in Vivi's direction, a mixture of frustration and irritation bubbling inside her. "I didn't know I needed to check in with you."

"You don't." Peter's voice stung. "But you do have to stay out of my official police investigation of the Brice Denman murder." Kate flinched at his tone but let him continue. "You had to go speak to Denman's ex-girlfriend, didn't you? Now she's so spooked, she won't talk to me."

When Peter's diatribe ended, Kate drew in a deep breath and let it out slowly. When she divorced Harry, she decided no man would order her around again. "What I don't have to do is listen to you talk to me that way. Goodbye." Kate hung up and without skipping a beat, placed a call.

Vivi raised her eyebrows. "Who're you calling?"

Kate smiled sweetly. "I've reconsidered that dinner invitation from Cole."

Nine

Kate slid a tube of frosted rose lipstick across her bottom lip, pressed her lips together, and stood back to survey the look. She'd exchanged the crocheted skirt set for a sleeveless, floral, cotton sundress before freshening her lipstick. Not bad for someone who'd left the house twelve hours earlier, held her own with the first lady and her daughter, lunched like the Austin elite, aggravated a cop, and spent more than six hours in the car. Her life in Texas was certainly not boring. Would her Stony Point friends recognize shy Kate these days?

The doorbell chimed, and Kate slipped on a pair of cream-colored pumps before walking to the door. She hesitated, her hand on the doorknob. *Am I doing the right thing, going out with Cole?* Peter seemed to think Cole was dangerous, but was he just jealous? *Am I doing this out of spite? That's almost as bad as jealousy.*

Questioning her own motive for accepting the dinner invitation she almost declined, Kate opened the door and nearly swooned when she saw Cole standing with his hands in the pockets of a lightweight camel-colored jacket, the green shirt beneath reflecting his hazel eyes. Despite the murder investigation hanging over his head, she was still attracted to him. "Hi, Cole." She stepped through the door and closed it behind her. "Any news?"

He shook his head. "No news." He waited until she put her keys in her purse and then took her hands in his. "I'd rather concentrate on you tonight, anyway. You're beautiful."

Kate felt warmth spread through her cheeks and stopped herself from deflecting the compliment as usual. "Thank you."

"No need to thank me for saying what's true." Cole led her down the front steps to the car. "I made us reservations at a little Italian place downtown. I asked the concierge at the hotel if he knew of a small, quiet restaurant with great food in Sage Hills. It turns out his sister lives here, so he knows about this place firsthand."

Kate knew the place but had never eaten there. The menu was creative but pricey, probably still less than what Cole was accustomed to paying for a nice meal in New York City. "Small and quiet is perfect. It's been a long day."

"I'm glad you're ending it with me." Cole opened the car door.

Kate slid into the car, and a wave of mixed feelings washed over her. She'd felt so safe with the musician she'd met in New York City, the man who swept her off her feet and poured his heart out to her in song. But that was before he was a prime suspect in a murder investigation. She'd had a dinner date with a suave businessman, Robert Townsend, earlier in the summer, and he ended up being a killer and a crook. Her record for choosing men wasn't too great—except when it came to Peter. And he could be overbearing at times.

Is it safe to be alone with Cole in a car, even if it is for a short distance? She pulled out her phone and texted Vivi to let her know where they'd be eating. She felt better knowing that someone else would know where she would be. She kept her phone in her hand until they pulled up to the canopied entrance of Bello's Ristorante.

Bello's was a small place accented with potted plants, subdued lighting, and flickering candles on each table. A classical guitarist strolled among the potted trees and tables, stopping every few minutes to serenade patrons with Italian songs. Kate was enchanted. "This is the perfect ending to an interesting day," Kate whispered to Cole as they followed the maître d' to a cozy corner table nestled between two ficus trees.

Once they were seated and their waiter, Bruno, had given them menus and taken their drink orders, Cole leaned closer to Kate. "I want to hear all about your interesting day."

Kate smiled. Harry had rarely asked about her day during their marriage. "Let's decide what to order first. Then I'll tell you about my visit with Sophia and Carolina Jackson."

By the time they decided, Bruno had reappeared with their water and iced tea. He gave them a rundown of the dinner specials before taking their order.

"Now, tell me about Austin," said Cole as Bruno scurried to the kitchen.

Cole didn't take his eyes off Kate as she recounted her experience at the Governor's Mansion. His eyebrows arched when she described the first lady's comments about the other designer, Marisa Sanchez. "It sounds like Mama is trying to run the show and the bride is rebelling. How did you handle it?"

He sat back in his chair when Kate explained how she glossed over Sophia Jackson's suggestion of another designer and refocused the conversation on her own designs without betraying her surprise. "So, you have the gig, and you beat out a designer known for creating looks for celebrities and the political elite?" Cole grinned. "You're not quite as shy as the Kate I met in the jazz club in New York City. I like it."

They reminisced about concerts, clambakes, and charity fundraisers they had attended during Cole's visits to Maine when they were getting to know each other. All of Kate's reservations about being alone with him dissolved. "Cole, what happened to us?"

"I don't know. Life sort of got away from me." He shook his head in disbelief. "I guess it was just one thing after another that got in the way—the band recorded a new album and gained national attention. Then came the tour."

Cole stopped talking and sipped his tea as Bruno arrived with a tray. He placed a plate of chicken cacciatore in front of Kate and a sizzling portion of veal Marsala before Cole. They declined a basket of bread.

When the waiter walked away, Cole resumed. "It's not easy to carry on a long-distance relationship." He stared into the candle flame. "Kate, what is it between you and Detective Matthews? Sparks nearly singe the two of you when you're in the same room together. And he seems protective of you."

Stalling for time, Kate sliced a bite of chicken and popped it into her mouth. "He's a cop. They do that," she said finally. "We've been out a few times. He's an incorrigible flirt, but there's nothing to it."

Cole raised his eyebrows and started to respond, but his words faded away when the strolling guitarist stopped at their table to sing. Relief swept over Kate. She was pretty sure she wasn't going to like the next words out of his mouth, and she didn't want to discuss Peter anymore. She much preferred drinking in the romantic atmosphere while listening to the music.

The musician strummed his guitar and sang with emotion in Italian, adding to the romantic atmosphere of Bello's. Kate couldn't help but think about how different the place was from The Spaghetti House, a restaurant where Peter had taken her to dinner a few months ago. Unlike the elegant Bello's, the family-friendly place had been casual and noisy, its tables filled with boisterous children and their parents. The food had been good, though, and she'd enjoyed the easy conversation with Peter.

Kate's thoughts bounced back and forth between Peter and Cole. Each man had asked about the other. She never thought she would have two attractive men battling for her attention. It shocked—and thrilled—her.

By the time the guitarist moved on, the music had worked its magic. Cole dropped the subject of Peter, and Kate found herself hoping the night would last a bit longer. He paid the check, and they walked out of the restaurant to a slight breeze gently moving tree branches under a starry sky.

Kate looked at the sky. "What a beautiful, clear evening."

"Yes, it is." Cole followed her gaze for a few seconds before looking down at her. "I noticed a park in the town center. Feel like a walk?"

"The perfect way to finish a lovely evening," Kate replied.

Halfway down the last block before the park, Cole took Kate's hand. "This is nice."

"Yes." Kate didn't know what else to say until they entered the park and saw the empty swings on the small playground past the gazebo. "Let's swing. I haven't been on a swing since Vanessa was little."

"I haven't been on one since I was a kid." Cole led her to the swing set and held a swing steady, waiting for her to sit before easing down onto the flexible, rubberized seat next to her.

Kate twisted from side to side by shifting her weight from one leg to the other, just like she had as a child. For a few minutes, she became little Katie again and reveled in the breeze lifting her hair as she twisted the swing as tight as possible before letting go and twirling until the chains were straight again. She hadn't giggled like that in years. When the swing was still, she realized Cole was staring at her, his upturned lips illuminated by the park lights.

"You're living your dream here, aren't you?" His voice was soft, almost caressing, like the summer breeze.

She sat for moment as the year flipped through her mind like the pictures in the old View-Master she had loved as a little girl. Vanessa was thriving in college both academically and socially while Kate was building a career in designing she had never thought possible. *I'm designing a wedding gown for the governor's daughter!* It all started because her friend and former boss in Maine, Mary Beth Brock, had enough faith in Kate's work that she secretly entered it in a national competition, and it won. It had taken someone else seeing her talent and forcing her to put it to the test. But while she'd had helping hands along the way, Kate knew she was changing, growing into a confident designer *and* woman.

"I never thought of it that way, but yes, I am living my dream." She pushed back with her feet and let go. The swing slowly moved back and forth. "I don't need fame and fortune. I just want to earn an honest living doing what I love, designing and crocheting. That's success to me."

Cole scuffed his feet across the rubber chips beneath the swings. "I think you're already successful."

"You are too."

"Maybe. Sometimes I feel successful. The university is happy with my work. I'm respected by students and faculty. I'm lucky enough to go on tour playing music I love, and I've even managed to record a few albums." He stopped talking and leaned back in his swing.

"But?"

"But sometimes I want to go for the big brass ring—a Grammy or an Oscar or a recording with a big-name musician." He straightened up and looked at Kate. "Do you think it's asking too much?"

"Not if that's what you really want and are willing to work for it," she said.

Kate waited for Cole to respond, but he sat wordlessly until Kate's cellphone cut the silence.

"Let me just make sure it isn't Vanessa." Kate dug the cellphone from her purse and groaned. "It's Peter."

Cole dipped his chin and looked away. Kate pushed the talk button on her phone. "Hi, Peter."

"Kate, are you OK? Your vehicle's at home but you and your cellphone aren't. Your phone shows you at the park."

Anger flashed through Kate's body. "Are you tracking me by my phone?"

"Now Kate—"

"Goodbye, Peter." She ended the call and turned off her phone. Kate slid off the swing and took a few paces. "He's tracking me."

Cole joined her, and they walked toward the water fountain at the center of the park." He stopped and turned to face her. "He's doing his job. I think the cop side of him wants to find the killer, and the infatuated side of him is looking out for you." Cole reached up and brushed the hair back from her face. "But I think his feelings for you motivated him to track and call you, not the murder case."

Several circles of water shot into the air from the center of the fountain, arched, and fell back into the pool with dainty splashes. Kate leaned over and ran the fingertips of her left hand through the water. "My ex-husband always treated me like I was stupid. Sometimes Peter acts like I can't take care of myself. Do I act that way?"

Cole gently grasped Kate's shoulder and turned her to face him. "Stupid and helpless are two words I'd never associate with Kate Stevens." She stood there frozen, her heart beating wildly in her chest, as he lowered his head to hers.

Out of the darkness in the street, a car squealed up to the curb, honking its horn and flickering its bright lights as Kate and Cole jumped apart and shielded their eyes. Cole grabbed Kate's hand and pulled her in the direction of the restaurant where he'd parked the car. "I think it's time to take you home."

"Yes." Kate wasn't sure if the pounding in her chest was from the surprise of bright lights and a honking horn or disappointment that the kiss didn't happen.

The walk back to the car was uneventful. Their talk was sporadic, but not uncomfortable. Kate knew they were both spooked by the mystery car in the park, but chances were it was a lost driver or mischievous teenager out for sport, not someone who meant them harm. But there was still a niggling thought. *What if it had something to do with Brice Denman's murder?*

Then it hit her—the only way to have any peace about Cole was to solve Brice Denman's murder. "Cole, I was planning on going to Dallas to look up Gwen's bachelorette friend and maybe find the music store. Want to go with me?"

He squeezed her hand. "I have an early morning phone call with Evan Klein about the investigation, but it shouldn't take long. There's not much to tell. Then I'm meeting with Gus at ten to discuss our options for the remainder of the tour. I could go after that."

"Good. I'll leave Sage Hills at ten. I should arrive at the hotel about the time your meeting is over. I hope to get three hours of design work done before I leave so I can spend the day away with a clear conscience."

With the Dallas trip settled, they listened to soft jazz music on the drive home. By the time Cole pulled up to Kate's house, her heart rate was back to normal. He jumped out of the car and loped around it to open Kate's door for her. Hand in hand, they strolled up the walkway to the front door. Her porch light cast a soft white glow over the steps. Her heartbeat ramped up again when Cole turned and placed his right hand on her face, his thumb caressing her cheek. "You are an amazing woman, Kate Stevens." His voice was husky. "Don't let anyone convince you otherwise."

Kate held her breath as Cole's lips brushed hers. She smiled when he lifted his head. "Thank you for tonight."

"It was most definitely my pleasure." Cole watched Kate unlock the door. "Want me to stick around a bit and make sure everything's OK?"

"I'm sure everything is fine, but thank you."

"Good night, then." He turned and walked down the steps.

Kate stepped inside the door but turned to watch Cole leave. Across the street, a truck pulled away from the curb in front of Vivi's house. She must have had an impromptu date. The truck and Cole's car disappeared down the street, and a shiver ran down her spine. *Who is leaving Vivi's house this late?* Kate had an urge to tell her friend about her conversation with Cole about their respective dreams as well as his thoughts about Peter's behavior. A yawn escaped her and her eyes became heavy. Perhaps it could wait until tomorrow.

Ten

Cole was waiting in the lobby of the Stay Suite Hotel when Kate entered through the electric sliding glass door. "Good morning," he said, bending to kiss her cheek. "Your timing is perfect. I just came down."

"I'm glad we're getting an early start." Kate shook the keys in her hand. "Maybe we'll have some answers by the end of the day."

"Answers would be good. Having this hanging over my head takes the fun out of performing. At least the club owner is being pretty good about the whole thing. Our shows will resume soon. But I'm concerned about my position at Columbia University. While any publicity, even negative, is profitable for the club, university officials want only positive press. The financial and legal ramifications aren't pretty, but since I'm already scheduled to be off for the fall semester, the university won't be associated with any of this." Cole started for the door. "Evan is trying to clear his schedule so he can fly down."

"I'm sorry, Cole. You don't deserve this. Neither do your bandmates."

"And Brice didn't deserve to die, either." Cole's face clouded. "We have to find out who did this. I'm convinced the cops are so busy trying to pin it on me that they aren't looking at anybody else."

"I think you're wrong. Even if Peter took an instant dislike to you or was jealous of our friendship, he'd never let it affect his work on an investigation. He wouldn't jeopardize his professionalism or career."

Kate pointed her key fob toward a row of fifteen-minute parking spaces just outside the entrance and clicked it. "I parked right there."

She was glad to see the cellphone attached to Cole's belt. Kate had left hers at home in case Peter tried to track her again. She was growing weary of his attitude. "I thought we could start with the hair salon where Gwen's bachelorette friend works. It's called Clip Art."

Cole cut his eyes at Kate as he opened the driver's-side door for her. "Gwen didn't tell us that."

"Ah, the miracles of modern technology. I searched her online. The salon has a pretty interesting website. I've already programmed the address on my GPS."

The route map popped up on the screen. Cole leaned over and peered at the streets on the map. "It looks like it's in the transitional section of Dallas, between the trendy business district and working-class neighborhood. We'll find a little bit of everything there." He looked at Kate's raised eyebrows. "I used to live here, remember? Plus, the band plays several gigs here a year."

"I forgot." Kate eased the van out of the parking place and into the street.

At the first red light, she turned on the car radio as the disc jockey transitioned from music to local news. Kate and Cole grew silent as the announcer mentioned her new hometown.

"Sage Hills police are addressing a growing problem of teenagers congregating in its downtown park at night," the announcer said. Cole turned up the volume on the radio. "Last night several teens were arrested for possession of alcohol. Three adult males were also arrested and charged with criminal mischief for spray-painting a swing set in the park. Sage Hills City Manager Roy Tullis expects the issue to be addressed at Monday's City Commission meeting."

Cole reached over and turned down the sound. "I guess that explains the pickup truck and its horn and headlights. It had nothing to do with Brice or the investigation."

"That's a relief." Kate stole a quick look at Cole before returning her eyes to the road. "I'm glad we left the park when we did."

"Me too," Cole replied.

Their conversation slowed as music and traffic commanded their attention. While Kate wasn't as familiar with Dallas as Fort Worth, she'd become an expert at maneuvering the vehicle through urban traffic. It wasn't long before the electronic voice announced, "Your destination is on the right." Kate scanned the storefronts. Clip Art was right where it was supposed to be.

Cole spied a parking place two doors down, and Kate slid into it with ease. "I hope she's working today," he said.

"I have faith." Kate put the van in park and unlocked the doors. "Let's go."

Clip Art was a narrow shop wedged between the Blue Bird Diner and an outdated women's clothing store. Posters hawking hair care products and trendy haircuts in rainbow colors lined the display window. A line of crinkled flyers, discarded cups, and newspapers found a final resting place on the ground against the front of the building.

A bell jangled when Kate and Cole entered the shop. Between the humming of blow-dryers, chatter, and the volume of techno music, the bells were pretty useless. They stood just inside the door and surveyed the shop until a hairdresser with shocking pink spikes looked up from the workstation closest to the entrance. "May I help you?"

Kate moved forward. "I'm here to see Angel Lauria."

The girl's eyes took in Kate's conservative appearance, her sleeveless white blouse and blue paisley skirt. "Do you have an appointment?"

"No, we just stopped in on the off chance she'd be free. But we can make an appointment, if necessary."

The hairdresser rubbed her index finger over the rhinestone on the side of her nose. "I'll go check."

Kate watched her disappear among the workstations, hairdressers, and clients. "I've never been in a place quite like this." She kept her voice low. "It's amazing what they do with hair these days. I go for a trim every eight weeks. That's about it."

Cole swept a strand of hair off Kate's bare upper arm and looked into her eyes. "I like your hair."

"I'm Angel." Kate looked up to find a stunning woman in her early thirties with dark features and sleek, chin-length black hair highlighted with bright red streaks. She didn't have any piercings, but a vivid tattoo of a colorful dragon snaked from just under her jaw line, down her neck, and onto her chest. "What can I do for you?"

"I'm Kate Stevens and this is my friend Cole Cutchins." She gestured at Cole.

It was Angel's turn to study Kate and Cole. Her eyes fixed on him. "You look familiar." Her gaze moved to Kate. "Are you cops?"

Kate smiled at the question. "No, but we are here to ask you a few questions about your bachelorette party." The hairdresser cringed, so Kate hurried to her question. "Was Gwen Wright there?"

"That's why you look familiar." Angel eyed Cole. "I saw your photo on the news. And now you're trying to clear your name."

He nodded. "Exactly. We're following leads and eliminating suspects until we find who killed Brice Denman."

"Gwen was one of your suspects?"

"She was," Kate answered. "Until we met and she told us about your bachelorette party. We just wanted to make sure it checked out."

"I've known Gwen since high school. She has plans for her future. A drug addict doesn't have a place in it, but she loved him. She'd never hurt him."

"We got that impression," Cole said. "Where was the party?"

"The Heartbeat. It's a neighborhood bar not too far from here. It wasn't a huge party, and everyone knew one other."

Kate studied Angel's tattoo. "Your tattoo is striking. The detail is so intricate. I'm a clothing designer, and I'd love to have a photo of the design." She pulled her camera from her purse. "Do you mind if I take a quick snap?"

"Sure." Angel lifted her chin to better display the tattoo. "What type of designing do you do?"

Kate described her work, mentioning her books and website.

"Cool." Angel seemed impressed. "I need to get back to work now. Good luck."

"Thank you," said Cole. He moved toward the door.

"Best wishes for your marriage." Kate joined him, and they left the salon.

"Somehow I can't quite see you with a dragon tattoo," Cole deadpanned as they strolled to the van.

Kate tossed her hair with dramatic flair. "You don't think so?"

"Nope. By the way, you realize she never gave a definitive yes or no about Gwen being at her party, don't you?"

"Yes. She volunteered information freely enough, but seemed to avoid giving us a direct answer. I guess that leaves us with a little more to do, doesn't it?" She looked past Cole and widened her eyes. "Yes! Look down the street. The Heartbeat. Suppose it's open this early?"

"Bars in this part of town are always open." Cole held out his arm and Kate grabbed it.

The Heartbeat wasn't a large, flashy place. It was early afternoon, and the bar was dark and nearly empty. A typical neighborhood bar, it offered the obligatory dartboard and pool table on one side and dark wood tables across the floor. The bar stretched along the back of the building. Mirrors and posters advertising various beverage companies decorated the walls.

While their eyes adjusted to the darkness, the bartender came out from behind the bar. "Can I help you?"

Kate pulled up the photo of Angel on her camera and held it out to him as he approached. "Did this woman have a bachelorette party here last Saturday?"

"Who wants to know?"

Cole stepped closer to the bartender. "We're on the trail of a killer, and we're clearing suspects one by one."

The bulky, blond bartender eyed them with suspicion. "Cops?"

"Hardly. I'm the number one suspect." Cole returned the man's stare. "We're trying to find out who killed a man linked to one of the women at the bachelorette party."

The bartender looked at the photo. "Yep, that's Angel. She's a regular. Her party was Saturday. What's she got to do with a murder?"

"Nothing." Kate gave him the photo of Gwen. "But this woman might. Was she at the party?"

He walked to the bar and held the photo under the hanging lights. "Yeah, she was here. Didn't drink like the others. Must have been the DD. She stuck it out until the end of the party, but I can't say she enjoyed it."

Kate shrugged. "DD?"

"Designated driver," Cole said.

"Oh." Kate felt the familiar blush creep up her neck. "About what time did she leave?" Kate returned the photos to her bag.

"It was around 2 a.m. They all left at the same time."

Cole nodded. "Is she a regular?"

"Nope. Some of the others from Angel's shop are, but not that one."

The outside door opened, and Kate turned to watch two middle-aged men walk straight toward the bar. "You've been a big help. Thank you."

"You're not going to sic the cops on me, right? I answered your questions for Angel, not the cops." The bartender lifted his finger to acknowledge the two men taking seats at the bar.

"No, if the cops come here, it'll be because someone else sent them."

Kate and Cole strolled out of the bar as the bartender greeted the customers. It was now after one o'clock. "Let's head to the music store and talk to the manager Gwen told us about," Kate said. "She said he was Brice's friend."

"Good Time Music. I remember that place. It's been there forever. It was here when I lived in Dallas."

"It's called Downtown Music now. I found it online." Kate stopped and pulled a notebook out of her purse. "The website said the manager's name is Dexter, no last name."

They continued to the van, and Kate unlocked it. "Can you find it from here?"

Cole looked doubtful. "I'm not sure. I don't remember this area at all."

Kate climbed into the driver's seat. "No worries. The GPS will get us there."

Downtown Music was about fourteen minutes away, in an area cleaner but more congested than the street where the salon and bar were located. They found a metered parking space a block away. "I hope this Dexter person can tell us more about Brice's connections in the music world," Cole said as he slipped several coins into the meter. "Someone must know who had it in for him."

One side of Downtown Music was devoted to instruments and sheet music. The other side offered CDs, a small selection of electronic equipment, and industry-related books and magazines. Cole steered them toward the equipment side, his eyes scanning for a manager.

A man with curly brown hair emerged from a door at the back of the equipment section. "May I help you?"

Cole came to a standstill. "It can't be."

"What?" Kate saw the shock on his face.

"Dexter Young. He was a student early in my teaching career at Columbia." His voice was a whisper. "Not a good one."

Dexter Young drew closer and the dawn of recognition in his eyes turned to a glare. "Well, if it isn't Cole Cutchins. Not so high and mighty now that you're a murder suspect, are you? I saw your photo on the news at the same time the reporter said Brice was killed with his own gun. Why aren't you in jail?"

Unsure of what to say, Kate kept her mouth shut and watched the two men.

"I read the newspapers," Dexter continued. "Can't say I'm surprised you killed Brice. You always were good at ruining lives." Dexter smirked. "I saw your show. Agreed with every word Brice yelled. All he did was speak the truth, and you killed him for it."

The muscles in Cole's face twitched. "I didn't kill Brice."

"Cut the act, Cutchins. You ruined that man's life every bit as much as you ruined mine when you kicked me out of the music program." He turned to Kate. "You should run while you can, lady. This man destroys people."

"Cole wouldn't—" Kate's words were eclipsed by Dexter's hatred.

"You don't think so?" The store manager spat out the words. "I couldn't get a gig with any decent band after he kicked me out of Columbia's School of Music. My chosen career rejected me." He slammed his fist on a shelf filled with amplifiers. "Now I'm stuck selling instruments to young musicians who actually have a shot at the big time because they weren't thrown under the bus by professors who were supposed to teach them."

Cole's mouth fell open. "Dexter, I'm sorry. But half the guys in my band never went to college, so that's not an excuse for not making it in the business. Besides, I didn't kick you out. I simply told you the truth. You weren't showing the discipline necessary to make it through the program or become an accomplished musician. You were skipping classes. I had no idea you stopped performing. I didn't even know you left New York. You could have stuck it out and tried harder. This is all on you, not me."

"Nobody would hire me after the great Cole Cutchins labeled me as a has-been that never was."

"I never called you that." Cole shook his head, his eyes flashing. "I never used that phrase."

His former student laughed. "Maybe not in those words, but the music world got the message loud and clear. This was the only place I could get a job. Fifteen years outfitting up-and-coming musicians. Know what that's like?"

Cole shook his head.

Dexter laughed again. "Of course you don't. Get out of my store. You're not welcome here."

The chance to ask about Brice was slipping away. Kate cleared her throat. "Mr. Young, please tell me about Brice Denman. His girlfriend said you two were friends."

"Yeah, we were united in our hatred for your boyfriend here." Dexter jabbed his finger in Cole's chest and then pointed at the shop door. "There's the door. Use it."

Cole put his hand behind Kate's elbow and propelled her toward the door. "Let's go."

Eleven

"Who was your late-night visitor Wednesday night?" Kate leaned on her broom as Vivi strolled up the walkway Friday morning. "I've been dying to know, but I was in Dallas with Cole most of yesterday."

Vivi cocked her head like a puppy confused by a voice command. "Kate, dear, what are you talking about?"

"When Cole brought me home after dinner, a dark truck pulled away from the curb in front of your house. I figured you had company."

"No. I stayed in alone and did paperwork. It's never ending." Vivi glanced across the street. "Peter's truck is dark. Maybe he was driving by to check on you. After all, you are mixed up in a murder investigation. He's probably worried about you."

Kate considered the idea. *It could have been Peter in the truck. Makes sense.* "Maybe so."

"On to more important things. Tell me about the music store manager. Do you think he's the killer?"

Kate recounted the previous day, glossing over the visits to the salon and bar to focus on Dexter Young. "He obviously has anger issues. He was hateful to Cole."

"Angry enough to kill Brice Denman and pin it on the man he claims ruined his life?"

"Maybe. He was certainly agitated."

Vivi bounced on her toes. "Want to go back without Cole and see if we can get him to talk?"

"Yes. But I really need to work on the wedding dress designs. I've been so preoccupied with investigating this murder that I've neglected my work."

Vivi's eyes drifted to her watch. "It's only nine thirty. Work for three hours, and I'll come back over. In the meantime, I'll see if I can dig up anything else on Dexter Young."

"Sounds good." Kate resumed the sweeping, grateful for Vivi's flexible schedule. She didn't want to confront Dexter Young alone.

"I'll drive this time." Vivi bounded down the walkway and turned to Kate when she reached the street. "I'll see you in three."

"The dude's playing the riff from Stevie Ray Vaughan's classic *Little Wing*. He can't be too washed up." Vivi watched Dexter Young's fingers fly over the strings of a red-and-white electric guitar on medium volume, her voice filled with admiration. "Are you sure this is the right guy?"

Kate and Vivi stood at the opening to the instrument section of Downtown Music watching Dexter demonstrating the guitar to a shaggy-haired teenage boy and a woman who appeared to be his mother. Dexter's fingers flew over the strings and his head bobbed to the beat as he tapped his foot. The sign above the line of guitars hanging on the wall behind them said "Fender Stratocaster." Kate recognized the name and wondered if the kid was a teen prodigy to be looking at a professional's guitar, or if Dexter was taking advantage of a chance to impress someone with his ability so he could sell him a higher-priced guitar. She determined it must be the latter.

"That's who Cole and I tried to talk with yesterday." Kate watched as Dexter finished the song, put the guitar on a stand, and talked to the teenager, his face aglow with excitement. "His demeanor is totally different today." She nodded toward the front of the shop. "Let's wait up front so we don't disturb them."

During the forty-five-minute drive from Sage Hills to Dallas, Vivi recounted the results of her research on Dexter Young. She found one drunk-and-disorderly incident report filed with the Dallas Police Department, a five-year marriage followed by a divorce finalized three years ago, and an article in an industry newsletter quoting him when the store expanded in 2005. He'd not led a charmed life, but there was nothing Vivi found even remotely suggesting he was capable of murder. Watching Dexter Young with the teen and his mother, Kate saw he did love music, and this was a bond he shared with his customers.

A few minutes later, the trio walked up to the cash register close to the entrance. The smiling boy was carrying a less flashy guitar. "Hone your skill on this, then come back to see me." Dexter punched the keys in the cash register and scanned the woman's credit card. "If you practice hard enough and really want it, eventually you'll be able to afford a Stratocaster."

The kid's lips just barely turned up as his eyebrows lifted.

The sale concluded, Dexter watched the mother and son leave the store before he turned to Kate and Vivi. "May I help—" His words stopped as recognition swept across his face. "You again."

Kate stepped forward and held out her hand. "I'm Kate Stevens. I didn't get a chance to introduce myself yesterday."

Dexter clasped her hand. "I'm not real proud of my behavior yesterday. A lot of memories flooded back when I saw Cutchins."

"I understand." Kate placed her hand on Vivi's arm. "This

is my friend Vivi. She's helping me try to figure out who killed Brice Denman."

Dexter acknowledged Vivi with a dip of his head and looked at Kate. "How can I help you prove who killed Brice?"

"Cole, Vivi, and I spoke with Gwen Wright on Tuesday. When we asked her if Brice had friends in the local music community, she mentioned you. We're trying to talk to anyone with a connection to him in hopes of uncovering who might have wished Brice harm." Kate fixed her gaze on Dexter's eyes. "Mr. Young, Cole didn't kill Brice. We're just trying to find out who did."

He returned her stare. "Why are you so interested in clearing Cole? Are you his girlfriend?"

"Just a friend, really. We met in a jazz club in New York City a couple of years ago. We reconnected when he came to town on tour."

"Wait. Are you *the* Kate from Cole's song?"

Kate dipped her head. "Yes."

"Some reunion you must have had." Dexter looked past Kate into the back of the store, his eyes glazed. A few seconds later he jerked his eyes back to Kate with a dawn of understanding. "You came to see me because you think I did it. You think *I* killed Brice."

"No. We came in looking for someone who might know if Brice had any enemies in the music scene here, someone who might have wanted him dead. I had no idea you and Cole knew each other until yesterday."

Vivi put her hands on her hips, tossed her head, and broke her silence. "You were at the club on the night Brice Denman was killed. That gives you opportunity. Given your obvious animosity toward Cole, the desire to pin a murder on him makes a pretty good motive."

"There won't be any of my fingerprints on the gun. I left the club through the front door and spent the night doing some serious soul searching." Dexter bent down behind the counter and disappeared from sight.

Kate was considering peeking behind it to check on what he was doing when Dexter stood up, placed several small boxes of guitar picks on the counter, and pushed them toward a small display of other impulse-purchase items. Then he walked around to the front of the counter and leaned back against it.

"I'll admit to some bad memories resurfacing after seeing Cole again at Charley's. When you came by here yesterday, I was faced with the reality of my own failure as a musician." His shoulders drooped. "But Cole was right. He never told me I didn't have talent, and he didn't kick me out of the program. He told me to decide if I was dedicated enough to do what it takes to make it in music. He'd looked me in the eye and said, 'If you are, then roll up your sleeves and get to work. If not, then get out and stop wasting my time.'" His eyes were moist, but tears didn't fall. "I quit."

Vivi and Kate exchanged a glance and waited for Dexter to compose himself and continue.

"I didn't kill or frame anyone. The only person I've hurt is myself. I walked away from the one thing that really mattered to me." He brushed both eyes and cleared his throat. "I do know someone who's mentioned getting even with Brice because—"

The shop door squeaked open and four men appearing to be in their twenties tromped through the door. "Dexter, dude. We got a hot gig in Houston next week, and idiot here blew up his amp last night." A scruffy, long-haired guy jabbed his thumb at a cleaner-cut young man behind him. "What can you do for us?"

Two others dressed from head to toe in loose-fitting

camouflage pants and jackets followed them. For a few seconds, Dexter's eyes bounced back and forth between the young men and Kate and Vivi. Finally, he motioned the women closer. "These guys are some of my best customers. I need to give them my undivided attention. Please come back. I might be able to help you. I close at five."

Kate and Vivi nodded in unison. "We'll be back," Kate said.

"Thank you for indulging my morbid curiosity," Kate said, studying the X marking the spot in Dealey Plaza where President John F. Kennedy was assassinated in 1963. She looked up and sighted the sixth floor of the Texas School Book Depository where Lee Harvey Oswald took aim on the president. Then her eyes traveled to the grassy knoll where some thought a second shooter fired another shot. "Somehow I expected a larger area."

"Most folks say that."

Vivi and Kate surveyed nearby tourists who were curious to see the place that would forever give Dallas a place in presidential history.

"A sad chapter in America's story was written here," Vivi said.

"My mom was fascinated with the Kennedys," Kate said. "I remember her talking about where she was the day Kennedy was shot."

Vivi pulled her gaze from a man with professional-looking camera equipment who was photographing the X. "Which was?"

"She was in fifth grade. Her class had just come in from recess when the principal announced it over the PA system. Mom said some kids were crying and others were worried the United States would get bombed by Russia since the president was dead. But she was also worried about Jackie Kennedy and her children." Kate looked at the X again. "Mom never had the money to come to Dallas, and she always regretted that. It was so personal for her."

Vivi looked at her watch. "If you want, I think we have time to stroll through the grassy knoll and go up to the Sixth Floor Museum to see the sniper's perch and maybe peek at a couple of exhibits before heading back to the music store. We can do it in your mom's honor."

They crossed the street to the knoll. Kate tried to envision the pandemonium and sense of shock witnesses experienced on the day the president was killed. Although only a child, her mother had listened to the radio broadcasts that day and had watched every televised anniversary show until the day she died. "Look at all the people here. Mom wasn't the only one fascinated by the intrigue surrounding JFK's death."

Kate and Vivi strolled to the open-air John F. Kennedy Memorial Plaza, entered the roofless concrete walls, and stared at the granite slab with the name of her mother's favorite president etched in gold. The monument was simple but powerful. The place left her feeling somber, and somehow she knew it would have made her mother feel the same way.

Then they walked over to the old Texas School Book Depository, entered the Sixth Floor Museum at Dealey Plaza, and stepped about five decades back in time. Kate soon became engrossed in the audio story and displays surrounding the day that had so intrigued her mother. She studied the storage area where a rifle was found after the shooting. It remained frozen in time, protected behind Plexiglass.

Kate shivered. "I'll never understand the world's preoccupation with guns."

"Sometimes guns are necessary, Kate."

"I don't know. There must be a better way to solve differences than with a gun." Kate thought of Cole's situation. "Brice Denman lost his life, and Cole's reputation, if not his freedom, may be in jeopardy because of a gun."

"Can't argue with you there," Vivi said, checking her watch. "Speaking of Cole, we need to get going. We're running late. We'll have to push it to get back before Dexter closes."

"I was afraid of this," Vivi said, resting her forehead on the knuckles of her hands and looking ahead to the long line of cars in front of her. "We stayed in the museum long enough to get caught in rush-hour traffic."

Friday often brought a mass exodus from the city as many fled the stress of urban living to seek refuge away from the city over the weekend. Kate was glad Vivi had offered to drive.

But each time Vivi tried to cut down a side street or try an alternate route, she found a traffic snarl. Kate watched the digits on the Mini Coop's clock change until it was only minutes away from five o'clock. Dexter would be closing the music store soon. *Will he wait for us?*

"This is crazy. I'm calling to ask Dexter to wait for us," Kate said, staring at the line of cars in front of them. She opened the notes app on her phone, found the number to the music store, and repeated it three times before closing the app and dialing. It rang several times before the voice mail picked up and a recording said it was past store hours and to please leave a message at the tone. Kate did as instructed. "Mr. Young, this is Kate Stevens. We were caught in traffic, but Vivi and I are on our way. Please wait for us. Thank you."

Vivi finally broke free of traffic about three blocks away from Downtown Music. It was 5:06. She eased into the first available parking place and they jumped out of the car to power-walk the last block to the store. Vivi trotted the last few steps to the door and tugged on it, despite the "Closed" sign hanging from the handle. "Ugh, I can't believe we missed him."

Kate peered in through the glass door. Most of the lights were off except for a bank of bulbs over the display windows. "He sure did a speedy lockup, especially since he told us to return."

"True." Vivi pursed her lips. "Maybe you struck a nerve when you told him you wondered if he might have set Cole up out of spite or revenge."

"There's only one way to find out," Kate said. "I guess I'll be getting to know Dallas a lot better before we solve this murder."

Twelve

Dexter was unlocking the door to Downtown Music the following morning when Vivi pulled her Mini Cooper into the parking place in front of the store. He looked up when she cut the engine.

"So you *are* interested," he said as Kate stretched a long leg out of the car. "I wasn't sure after you didn't show up yesterday."

"We just missed you." Kate stepped onto the sidewalk. "Dallas traffic."

"I left right at closing time. Had a lot on my mind." He dipped his chin. "Give me a minute to turn off the alarm, and then you can come in. I'll get you when it's all clear." He disappeared into the store. Sixty seconds later, the store was aglow with light and he reappeared at the door. "Come on in. We have time to talk before things get crazy."

Kate and Vivi followed Dexter to the register counter. He walked behind it, switched on the computer, and gestured for the women to follow him. "Please, sit down," he said, waving his hand to offer them two of the three stools.

"Thank you for talking with us again." Kate slid onto the middle stool.

"Seeing Cole forced me to take an honest look at myself. It wasn't pleasant, but it was necessary." His eyes drifted from Kate to Vivi. "I doubt I'd have faced my past if you hadn't been so persistent. Thank you."

Kate smiled. Persistence and self-confidence were traits

she'd worked hard to develop after her divorce, especially since moving to Texas and creating a new life for herself. She was pleased if she could help someone else conquer their own demons. "Mr. Young, what were you going to tell us?"

He pulled his stool directly in front of the women and sat on it, leaning forward with his hands on his thighs. "I was saying that I do know someone with an ax to grind with Brice."

"Who?" Vivi tapped her shoe on the lowest rung of her stool.

Dexter hesitated a minute, and Kate feared he had second thoughts. Relief coursed through her body when he finally began to speak. "A regular customer of mine was harping about Brice stealing her songs, making recordings, and posting them online as his own."

Vivi whistled. "That sounds like motive to me."

"Yeah, she said she'd find a way to get even with him. I figured she'd slam him on music blogs and stuff—you know, to discredit him. She badmouthed him all over Dallas-Fort Worth to anyone who'd listen. Online seemed like the obvious next step."

"Maybe murder was the next step," Vivi said.

"Could be." Dexter scooted his stool closer to the computer and tapped on the keyboard. A few seconds later he jotted down information from the screen onto the back of a Downtown Music Store business card and held it out to Kate. "Her name is Chyna Moody. She fronts a rock band called Broken Chyna. Don't call the cops because she's a scrapper and will either retaliate or run. She won't tell you a thing if she thinks cops will be involved. Chyna's a talented musician, but she's had a rough life."

Kate slid the card into the side pocket of her purse. "Does she live near here?"

He shook his head. "Not close by, but she's in Dallas."

The store door opened, and Dexter stood up to greet the customer. "You can stay here. I'll see what he needs." He walked toward the front of the shop where the customer stood hidden from Kate's view behind a display sign. "What can I do for you?"

"I'm Detective Peter Matthews, Fort Worth PD." Kate and Vivi exchanged a look, their eyes wide with surprise. "I believe you have a couple of visitors here."

Peter was clipping his badge to his belt when he stepped up to the register counter. "Good morning, ladies." Peter's scowl didn't match the friendly tone in his voice. "I'd like you to wait outside while I speak with Mr. Young."

Peter was dismissing them like children. Kate glowered back at him. She didn't budge. Neither did Vivi.

"So that's how you're going to play it?" Peter sauntered behind the counter, grabbed each by an arm, and escorted them to the door. "You stay out here. I'll deal with you later."

"Don't bother coming back in, Detective. I don't talk to cops." Dexter's words were shouted at Peter's back. Kate knew that wouldn't do any good. In fact, the words had just made Peter smile.

He opened the door and eased the women through it. "I'll only be a minute."

"Maybe not that long." Vivi grinned. "Dexter didn't seem too glad to see you."

"You let me worry about Dexter. Stay out of trouble for a few minutes." He stepped back through the door and pushed it closed behind him.

Vivi moved out of the doorway and leaned against the store's brick wall. "My guess is our friend Dexter won't tell him anything about Chyna Moody. I don't think we should, either. He's really steamed at us right now."

"I agree." Kate yawned. She hadn't slept well since she first learned Cole was suspected of Brice Denman's murder. The lack of sleep and the stress were beginning to take their toll on her. "I think we need to wait on our visit to Chyna. Peter might follow us, plus I need to catch up on my design work."

"I know you thought you were moving to a sleepy little village, but you haven't gotten much rest since you moved," Vivi said. "It won't hurt to let the police department do its job while we take a short break."

Before long, Peter emerged from the music store. He crossed his arms and peered at the women through narrowed eyes. "I see Vivi's car but not yours," he said to Kate. "So, I assume you rode with her."

Kate lifted her head. "Yes."

"Your phone's at home. Imagine how surprised I was when I arrived in Sage Hills and you weren't there—again."

Kate had expected Peter to trace her phone, but she wasn't about to let him know it. She didn't know what to say, so she opted to stay silent.

"Peter, we're only trying to help." Vivi filled the silence. "After all, Cole is Kate's friend."

"A friend, I might add, who is possibly facing a murder charge. Have you forgotten that?" Peter's voice was tinged with exasperation. "Texas Penal Code, section thirty-eight, subsection fifteen: interference with a police officer."

"What?" Vivi asked.

"That is what I could charge both of you with. Would you like me to quote chapter and verse?"

"Of course not," Kate said. "But I can't just sit around and wait for something to happen."

Peter shook his head. "You two will be the death of me yet. Vivi, why don't you head on back to Sage Hills alone? I'd like to treat Kate to lunch and catch up on things."

Vivi put her hands on her hips. "Don't you think you should ask Kate first?"

"Will you two please stop talking about me like I'm not here?" Kate looked Peter in the eye. "Lunch would be nice—*if* you don't spend the entire time telling me what I can and can't do. I am not a child."

His lips curved into his charmingly crooked smile. "I'll do my best to behave."

"I guess I'll head back to Sage Hills then," Vivi said. "I do need to get ready for work anyway. We have an event at the hotel tonight."

"I'll be fine. Thanks." Kate stood up straight. "I'll call you tomorrow."

Vivi unlocked her car and slid behind the steering wheel. Kate watched her drive down the street before giving her attention to Peter. The day had taken an unexpected turn. She was glad she'd chosen to wear the flirty, apricot floral-and-lace dress she'd made last summer. It was an appropriate weekend lunch outfit. "Did you have a particular lunch spot in mind?"

"Not really. I thought we'd check out the arts district. It's still a little early for lunch. There are several great restaurants in the area." He stood back and grinned. "You look great, by the way. We'll just walk around until something jumps out at us."

"Sounds like a good plan." Her hand bumped Peter's, and she was startled when he grabbed it, intertwining his fingers in hers.

They walked hand in hand down the block to Peter's Taurus. Given her attire, Kate was glad he was driving the sedan and not his huge pickup truck. He unlocked the car door and held it open for her, something her ex-husband Harry had never done. He'd always jump in the car first and turned the key in the ignition before she reached her door. While Kate enjoyed her newfound independence, she also liked being treated like a lady. She wasn't happy about the way Peter had barged into the music store and pushed them outside, but she had to admit to herself that the thought of spending the afternoon with him made her stomach flutter. She hoped the lunch conversation wouldn't be about murder and Cole.

As they neared the arts district, Kate began recognizing streets Vivi had taken, trying to avoid traffic snarls on their way back to the music store the previous day. Peter found a parking space along Flora Street between Pearl and Olive streets. They strolled down Flora Street to Pearl Street so Kate could see the Belo Mansion.

"It was built in the 1880s by newspaperman Alfred Horatio Belo," Peter explained as Kate stood in awe of the stately landmark. "It was a funeral home in the 1930s. Now it's home to the Dallas Bar Association."

The columns of the Belo Mansion reminded Kate of the Governor's Mansion. She realized she'd never told Peter about her meeting with the first lady of Texas and her daughter. "This reminds me, I never told you why Vivi and I went to Austin."

"No, as a matter of fact, you didn't," Peter said. "You've been too busy spending time with Cole and playing amateur sleuth."

Kate took a deep breath and was about to volley a defense until she saw the mischievous twinkle in his eye. She slowly exhaled and smiled. "It was quite the experience, my visit with Sophia and Carolina Jackson. I'll tell you all about it during lunch."

"Ah, the governor's wife and daughter. Won't you give me a hint?"

"Nope. A little anticipation is good for the soul." Kate grinned.

"I've been experiencing too much anticipation since I met you." He grimaced. "But I guess I can handle it."

Kate threw back her head and laughed. It felt good to banter with Peter. "You'll get used to it."

"I hope not," he deadpanned.

They walked a block down Ross Avenue and turned onto Harwood Avenue, heading toward the Dallas Museum of Art. "It's really something," Peter said, stopping to study the building. "We'll come back sometime and go through it. Right now my stomach is growling."

They cut back to Olive Street as Peter described the restaurant he had in mind for lunch. The Big Sky Restaurant was owned by Chris Weaver, a kid from his old neighborhood who'd paid his way through culinary school working in some of the best restaurants in Dallas. He'd opened the Big Sky about three years earlier. Both trendy and comfortable, the place was known for its creative menu. "It's one of the hottest places in town now." Peter's voice was filled with pride for his childhood friend. "It's gratifying to see a good person rewarded for hard work."

The Big Sky Restaurant wasn't large, but the blue-and-silver decor made the place look bigger. Communal seating filled the center of the space, and smaller U-shaped booths offered privacy. Kate hadn't seen anything quite like it. Peter requested a booth at the hostess station and soon they were sliding into one of their own.

"Do you trust me to order for you?" Peter looked into Kate's eyes as the waiter dashed to the drink station for iced tea and water. Allowing Peter to select her lunch seemed important to him.

Kate hesitated. She'd spent several years learning how to think for herself and finding the courage to do it. Would letting Peter order for her make him think she was giving him control over her life? But Peter and Harry were two different types of men. She couldn't let the past determine her future.

"Yes, I trust you," she said, returning his gaze.

"Good to know." He smiled and the creases beneath the corners of his eyes deepened.

The waiter returned with two glasses of water and a pair of tall iced teas. Peter ordered smoked salmon with caper butter over wild rice and a ribeye steak served atop sautéed spinach and capped with rounds of black truffle butter. "You'll have to try a little of each. I can't decide which I like best," Peter said after the waiter left.

Peter slid closer to Kate in the curve of the booth. "Kate, I'm concerned about you leaving your phone at home." His voice was steady but his eyes were gentle. "It's dangerous for you to be out without it. A cellphone can be a lifeline if you need help. I hope you didn't leave it at home on purpose."

"And what if I did? What legal right do you have to hone in on my cell signal and track my activities?" Kate asked. "It's stalker behavior."

"You think I'm stalking you? It might be good for you to remember that I helped you avoid someone who *was* stalking you." Peter had indeed helped Kate when a cyber-stalker had kidnapped her and threatened her life. "You're spending a lot of time with a person of interest in a murder. Did you ever think that I might have someone following Cole? How am I supposed to ignore that you're very close to aiding and abetting a suspected felon?"

Kate was glad the booth was lit mainly by candlelight as a burning blush crept up her neck. "I'm just addled by Cole being in town and suspected of murder." Would he notice she hadn't addressed his comment?

He took a sip of tea and stared into the glass for several seconds before turning to Kate. "I'm getting a lot of heat from the brass to arrest Cole and close this case."

Heaviness hit Kate's stomach. "Why?"

"We have motive, opportunity, and a witness placing him at the scene." Peter rubbed the side of his face. "And the owner of Charley's is a friend of the mayor. Evidently, customers are afraid to go to the club now. The mayor is a powerful man." Peter took Kate's hands in his. "I don't want you caught in the crossfire of this case. Please leave the investigation to me. I'll keep you as informed as I can."

Kate considered his words and his tenderness in delivering them. Could she keep a promise to stay out of the investigation?

The waiter arrived with their food stacked on a series of plates lining each arm. She'd never been so happy to see a server in her life. "Thank you," she said as he placed the salmon in front of her. "Everything looks delicious."

He nodded. "Is there anything else I can do for you?"

Peter declined, and the waiter backed away from the table.

Kate took a bite of salmon. "This is so good, it's decadent. Want a taste?"

They exchanged samples of Peter's steak and Kate's salmon. Kate was tempted to tell him he could order for her anytime.

Peter cleared his throat. "Kate, I meant what I—"

"Oh!" Kate interjected before Peter could return back to the topic of Cole and the investigation. "I was going to tell you about my trip to Austin. It was quite amazing."

"Do tell," Peter said, slicing a big bite of steak and popping it into his mouth.

Relieved, Kate recounted the meeting—and friction—with the first lady and her daughter as well as the conversation overheard at the next table during lunch at The Driskill. Peter raised his eyebrows at Kate's description of the Jacksons' behavior and smiled at her reaction to it.

"You're designing a wedding dress for the governor's daughter." Peter bobbed his head in approval. "Be prepared. After this wedding, you will likely have more business than you've ever imagined."

Gentle warmth spread through Kate, but this time it wasn't from embarrassment. Peter's words filled her with hope for the future. "I hope you're right."

"I am." Peter's voice oozed with confidence. "Believe me."

A glow settled over her on the drive back to Sage Hills. They chatted easily about the potential for the Dallas Cowboys to get to the Super Bowl and Vanessa's upcoming sophomore year at Regency College—anything but Cole and the investigation.

When Peter pulled the Taurus up to the curb in front of Kate's house, he jumped out and trotted around the car to open her door, offering his hand to her as she rose from the seat. They strolled hand in hand up the sidewalk to the porch. When they reached the door, Peter turned to her, his eyes searching hers. The memory of Cole's kiss flickered though her mind, followed by Vivi's suggestion that Peter might have been watching her house at the time.

"Kate? What is it? You have a funny look on your face."

Kate's heart thumped wildly in her chest. "Peter, were you watching my house Wednesday night? It was dark, but I saw a truck drive off when Cole and I came home from dinner."

She stepped back and waited for his answer.

"Just keeping an eye on it for your safety. That's all." He stepped closer. "Kate, I won't lie to you. It was difficult to watch you kiss another man. There's a part of me that's jealous of this suave New York musician vying for your affection, but it won't interfere with the investigation. I want to find out who killed Brice Denman because it's my job. It won't change my feelings for you, either. I promise."

He bent down and brushed her lips with his. "I enjoyed our day, Kate."

"I did too. Thank you." She kissed his cheek, happy they'd gotten the Cole issue out in the open. "I'm sorry I gave you such a hard time about my phone. I know you're only doing your job. You're a great cop."

Peter grinned. "You're not so bad yourself." He kissed her again, his lips lingering a little longer, before turning to leave. "Good night, Kate."

Kate stood on the porch and watched him drive away, her thoughts muddled. *How can I have feelings for two men who are so different?*

Thirteen

On Monday morning, Kate sat at her drafting desk, sipping chamomile tea and slowly flipping through the series of wedding dress designs she'd sketched for Carolina Jackson. Despite the trips to Austin, Fort Worth, and Dallas, she'd found pockets of time to work on the collection.

The creative challenge had been to find ways of blending elements of the Southern belle style favored by Sophia Jackson with the sleek lines of the mermaid style her daughter desired. The result was a portfolio of eight drawings, three of which achieved this balance between styles. Three designs focused only on the bride's taste, and the remaining two, created with the mother of the bride in mind, featured billowy, sheer sleeves and layers of lace on a flowing skirt.

She leaned back in her chair and considered the selections she had to offer the Jacksons. She was pleased with all of them, but her favorite was a sleek mermaid-style dress with a small, sheer train. It featured a V-neck, plunging back, and a magnolia-blossom-and-leaf design. Would any of these dresses please both mother and daughter? Kate wouldn't allow herself to think of what might happen if the bride chose none of her designs. The thought gave her an idea for her monthly magazine column in *Hook and Needle Arts*—creative compromise in designing crochet wear. It also made her consider whether or not to get a second opinion before showing the designs to the Jacksons.

She grabbed her phone from the edge of the design desk

and dialed Paige Bryant's number. Without mentioning the governor's family directly, Kate told Paige the wedding planner she had met at Once Upon a Yarn had contacted her about designing the wedding dress for a well-to-do client. "Do you have time to take a quick peek at the sketches this afternoon? I'd like a second set of eyes to see them before the family does."

Paige chuckled. "Kate, your design work far surpasses mine, but I'd give anything for the opportunity to see the sketches before the mother of the bride!"

"Don't sell yourself short, Paige. Your opinion means a lot to me," Kate replied. "I need to call Vanessa and check on her schedule. Then I'll head to Fort Worth. I'll be there in an hour or so, depending on how much time Vanessa has to chat."

"No problem. I'll be here until five o'clock," Paige said. "See you soon."

After ending the call with Paige, Kate immediately dialed Vanessa. She hadn't talked to her daughter since summer final exams were over. The conversation was short, as Vanessa was packing up her dorm and preparing to go to Joe Pool Lake in Grand Prairie for a few days with her suitemates Maddie and Zoe.

"I'll drop a load of stuff by the house before we head to the lake this afternoon." Vanessa sounded breathless from packing. "Will you be home?"

"Should be." Kate snapped off the light over her desk and picked up her portfolio. "I'm getting ready to go to Fort Worth to show Paige some sketches, but I won't be long. Do you have much to store?"

"Not much, just a few boxes. We can stack them in the corner of the studio. There's no sense in unpacking them when I'll be going back so soon."

"Sounds good. I'm glad you have time to relax with your

friends before starting fall classes." Kate put her portfolio on the kitchen table and walked back to the bedroom to slide into her sandals. "Thanks for filling me in. I'll let you go."

"Oh, Mom, wait. How's everything with Cole and the investigation? I haven't seen anything in the paper for a few days. Anything new?"

"Not really. Vivi, Cole, and I are running down some leads, but we don't have anything concrete yet. Luckily, Cole hasn't been arrested." Kate didn't want to mention Peter's comments about the mayor wanting an arrest soon. "I'll keep you posted."

"Thanks, Mom. I love you."

"I love you too. See you this afternoon." Kate signed off and smiled. She treasured these visits with her daughter.

"These wedding dress designs are absolutely scrumptious," Paige said, flipping through Kate's portfolio for the third time. They were sitting in two of the four chairs surrounding the coffee table at Once Upon a Yarn. "A bride would be beautiful in any of them."

She cocked her head at Kate. "By the way, who's the bride?"

Kate bit her lip. She hadn't exactly been told to keep it under wraps, and she had let Peter in on it. "I'd tell you, but then I'd have to kill you," Kate joked.

Paige laughed and didn't push the issue. "You and Sherlock Holmes, huh?"

"Something like that." Kate smiled. "After all, I *have* stumbled into my share of mysteries since moving to Texas."

"That's for sure." Paige flipped back and forth between the

pages of Kate's portfolio. "You have two distinctly different looks here, and three sketches that combine them. Why these styles?"

"You caught me." Kate leaned over and turned pages to find the sleek, mermaid-style dresses. "These are the types of dresses the bride wants to wear." She turned several more pages. "And these are variations of the style her mother repeatedly told her she should wear."

"You are a master of diplomacy," Paige said. "I hope this commission leads to more bridal work for you. You have a knack for it."

"It could, if I can please both mother and daughter." Kate closed her portfolio and stood up. "Or it could put the brakes on it before I even get started. We'll see."

A pang of guilt hit Kate when she spied the almost-empty dress form waiting for the sheer, floral-lace shirt she'd designed, then put aside when the Jacksons summoned her to Austin. Paige had draped an airy lavender shawl around the shoulders. "I'm sorry I haven't gotten the shirt done for you. Life's been a bit hectic lately."

Paige rose from her chair and gave Kate a hug. "If all goes well with the wedding dress, and I believe it will, I've a feeling you'll soon be even busier. Don't worry about the shirt until you finish the wedding dress."

"Thanks for the compliment and your faith in my work. Now I need to get back home. Vanessa is stopping by on her way to Joe Pool Lake." Kate gathered her portfolio and purse and walked toward the door. Halfway to the front of the shop, she turned to Paige and grinned. "I promise to let you know who the client is as soon as I can."

On the way home, Kate stopped in Murray's Market to pick up a couple of chicken breasts, a pair of baking potatoes, and a head of romaine lettuce, just in case she could persuade Vanessa to delay her departure to the lake long enough to have dinner. If not, then it would be nice to have leftovers.

Dressed for the lake in a sleeveless blouse and shorts, Vanessa was sitting in the living room, watching TV, when Kate unlocked the front door, balancing her portfolio under one arm and a grocery bag in the other. Vanessa sprinted to the door as soon as her mom was inside. "Let me help you, Mom." She took the bag and carried it through the living room to the kitchen. Kate placed her portfolio on the coffee table and followed her daughter. When she reached the kitchen, Vanessa was already pulling items out of the bag.

"Two chicken breasts, two potatoes, and lettuce. Do you have a dinner guest coming?" Vanessa sounded hopeful. "Peter or Cole?"

"Neither," Kate said, attempting to keep her voice and face neutral.

"Mom, is there someone else I don't know about?" Vanessa stood unmoving, hands on hips, until Kate cracked a smile. "You're becoming quite the belle of the ball around here."

"No, sorry." Kate moved the potatoes and lettuce to the counter by the sink and put the chicken in the refrigerator. "I stopped by the store on the way home just in case you had time to share dinner with me before leaving town."

Vanessa's face fell. "I wish I could, but Maddie and Zoe will be by to pick me up in a little while. I hope it's OK if I leave Fred here." Vanessa had affectionately named the Ford Fusion that Harry had purchased for her sixteenth birthday.

"Of course it's fine. I'll take good care of him." Disappointed that Vanessa wouldn't be staying for dinner, Kate fought to appear cheerful as they returned to the living room. "I hope you girls have a great time. You deserve it."

They'd just entered the living room when a horn beeped three times. Kate looked out the window as a beige older-model SUV came to a stop in front of the cottage. "I see your chariot awaits."

"I'll take a rain check on dinner. We'll have a week or so before classes to catch up." Vanessa hugged Kate before grabbing the backpack and canvas bag she'd left by the front door. "I love you, Mom. Good luck with those two gorgeous men."

Kate stood in the doorway and waved to Vanessa's suit-emates as her daughter loped down the walkway to the SUV, her long ponytail bouncing behind her. She laughed when she heard a duet of "We love you, Mrs. Stevens!" filter through the air. Kate cupped her hands to her mouth. "Love you too!"

When the vehicle disappeared from sight, Kate closed the door and returned to the kitchen. Happy to be home, with or without Vanessa, she decided to fix the entire meal anyway. If nothing else, she'd have a meal ready when she returned from Austin on Wednesday. For the first time in her life, Kate found enjoyment in puttering in the kitchen, even preparing something as simple as lemon pepper chicken, a baked potato, and salad. She didn't have to plan around Vanessa's social life. She was her own woman now. Peaceful satisfaction flowed through her.

When the chicken and potatoes were in the oven, she tore the lettuce and put it in the refrigerator. She was debating whether to work on her next magazine column or the piece she was crocheting for Paige's shop when her cellphone rang. It was Cole, and for a split second she wondered if it would be best to let the call go to voice mail and enjoy her peaceful silence, but she answered it anyway.

"Hi, Cole. How are you?"

"I'm OK. I just had to get out. The investigation has me unnerved. Do you mind if I stop by?"

"Of course I don't mind. Come on by." Kate wasn't sure if she really minded or not, but this would give her a chance to tell him about the return trips she and Vivi had made to see Dexter. "In fact, I have some information from Dexter for you. Vivi and I went back to see him. He told us about another possible suspect. I'll give you details when you arrive. How soon will you be here?"

"About ten minutes."

"I'll see you then." Kate ended the call and slid her phone onto the kitchen table.

Soon the chicken would send a lemony aroma into the air, and Cole would know she had dinner in the oven. Should she invite him to stay for dinner? What if Peter called or stopped by and discovered his murder suspect once again on her doorstep? As she wiped the kitchen counter, Vanessa's teasing words echoed in her mind. *You're becoming quite the belle of the ball around here.* Her daughter watched too many Disney movies. Kate was no princess. She smiled at the irony. The two men most interested in her were the cop who investigated her as a person of interest in a murder the first time she visited Texas and the man he apparently believed was a murderer. A memory of a long-ago conversation with Harry crept into her mind unbidden.

"You think life will be so great without me?" He'd spat the words at her when he was stone-cold sober and they were finalizing their divorce. "You'll die a lonely old woman." But Harry had been wrong. Even without the attention of two attractive men, she had friends she could count on. And she had Vanessa. Kate was blessed with people who cared about her, whether or not Harry believed it.

She didn't know where her relationships with Peter and Cole would lead, but the most important thing was that she knew she'd do just fine without a man, if that was how her life turned out.

The doorbell rang, and Kate shook the memories out of her head and answered the door. Cole was devastatingly handsome in blue jeans, a black ribbed pullover, and worn loafers. She opened the door wider and backed away. "Hi. Come in."

He kissed her cheek as soon as she closed the door. "Hmmm, what smells so good?"

"Are you referring to my perfume or the lemon pepper chicken baking in the oven?" She was interested to see if he was wrangling a dinner invitation or simply flirting. Maybe both.

"Yes." He grinned. "Seriously, thanks for letting me come over. I'm sorry I haven't been around much lately. We're trying to honor our contract with the club. The turnout has been as high as usual because of the publicity surrounding the murder, but they still don't like the association. They're getting a little testy. Cops and reporters won't leave us alone. I've been trying to wrap my head around it all."

"I can only imagine." Kate motioned for him to sit down in the love seat and joined him there. "I'm sure it hasn't been easy hearing some of the things people have said about you."

Cole drummed his fingers on his thighs. "It's not easy, but it helps knowing good people believe me—you, Vivi, Evan, and the Denmans. It's important to me that the Denmans believe me."

"I think Dexter believes you too." Kate described her two return trips to Downtown Music with Vivi. "I think he regrets blaming you for his problems all these years, not to mention the hateful things he said to you. At first I thought maybe he'd killed Brice and set you up to take the blame, but now

I'm not so sure. At any rate, Peter's talked to him, although he didn't tell me the details of the conversation."

"So, who is this new suspect Dexter mentioned?"

"Her name is Chyna Moody. She's a singer-songwriter."

Cole looked confused. "The name doesn't ring a bell."

"She doesn't exactly play your kind of music." Kate smiled. "I think hers is described as alternative rock."

Kate recounted Dexter's story about Chyna Moody accusing Brice of stealing her songs. "It could be a motive for murder, don't you think?"

He nodded. "If it's true, yes."

Kate stood up. "I have an idea. Wait here." She retrieved her laptop from her studio and returned to the love seat. "Let's see if we can find some of Brice's videos."

She went to a music video site and typed "Brice Denman" into the search box. There were five Brice Denmans listed. Cole's former bandmate was fourth on the list. The first of Brice's three songs was a cover of a recent Billboard chart topper. The second was a rock classic. Kate and Cole listened to a verse in each.

Cole closed his eyes as Brice held out the last note of the Eagles classic hit, *Already Gone*. He grimaced. "I wish you could have heard Brice sing before he found drugs."

At a loss for words, Kate clicked on the third song, entitled *Painful Passion*. They listened as Brice played the piano and sang the gut-wrenching lyrics, neither speaking until the video stopped, freezing Brice's image onscreen. "It says he wrote that."

Cole shrugged. "Could be Chyna's song, I suppose. It's good. Not my style of music, but it's good."

Kate pulled her eyes from Brice's face and looked at Cole. "Good enough to kill for?"

Cole was clenching his jaw so tightly Kate could see his neck muscles bulging. "Kate, we have to find out who killed Brice before they throw me in jail for something I didn't do. When do you plan to visit Chyna Moody?"

The desperation in Cole's voice startled her. His situation was serious, but if he was innocent, everything should work out in the end. "I'm tied up with work commitments tomorrow. I'll be in Austin on Wednesday, but I'll make it a priority for Thursday."

"I'm counting on it," Cole said. "I think my life depends on it."

His words sent a chill down Kate's back. She was uncomfortable being responsible for someone else's life.

The timer on the oven chimed, and Kate welcomed the chance to leave the room and change the course of the conversation. "I'll be right back. Don't move." She pulled the chicken and potatoes out of the oven and placed the pan on the stove before grabbing the greens and salad dressing from the refrigerator. Taking a deep breath, she stuck her head in the living room. "Would you like to stay for dinner?"

"Yes," Cole said. "I'd like that very much."

"One caveat—no more talk about murder or police investigations." Kate raised her eyebrows. "Deal?"

Cole nodded. "Deal."

Fourteen

The following morning, Kate started her day early, relieved to have the wedding dress designs ready for tomorrow's meeting with the Jacksons and determined to put the drama of Cole and Peter out of her mind.

She devoted the morning to reading and answering email, updating her social media accounts, and returning a couple of phone calls, one to her agent, Adam Vargas, and another to a local needlecraft club president who'd asked if she'd be a guest speaker at one of the group's fall meetings. Kate accepted the invitation, although she experienced a brief panic after hanging up the phone. She spent the next forty-five minutes searching the Internet for public-speaking classes at local colleges, then emailing requests for more information from six of them. *Maybe being prepared for speaking engagements will make them less intimidating.*

She stopped for lunch around one o'clock. As had become her habit since living alone, Kate sat at the table and read while munching leftover chicken and salad. Swept up in the thrilling horse racing world of the mystery novel Vivi had loaned her, she was surprised when she looked at the kitchen clock and saw an hour had passed.

Kate returned to her studio to brainstorm her next few blog posts, grateful to Alexus Lauren, her book editor at Brighton & Craig Publishing, for showing her how to write and post them in advance with scheduled publishing dates. She picked up her cellphone to move it off a pile of papers and was surprised to see she'd missed a phone call. She dialed her voice mail to listen to the message.

"Mrs. Stevens, I'm calling for Mrs. Jackson, who regrets to inform you she must cancel the review of bridal dress design ideas scheduled for 11 a.m. tomorrow. Thank you."

Kate saved the message and stared at the phone. The caller hadn't identified herself and the number was listed as "Unavailable." Odd. The message didn't contain an alternate date or a request to reschedule.

Kate dialed Jamie Martin's number, the only contact she had at the Governor's Mansion. Perhaps she could double-check the cancellation and, if necessary, reschedule the design review. A few seconds later, Kate exhaled with frustration when Ms. Martin's voice mail picked up the call. She left a message asking for confirmation of the 11 a.m. dress design review appointment.

Kate was confident Ms. Martin would return her call. In the meantime, if the meeting was cancelled, it provided time to locate Chyna Moody a day earlier than planned, and that was a good thing. The faster Brice Denman's murder was solved, the sooner she could concentrate on her career.

The afternoon passed quickly, and by four o'clock she'd checked off every item on her to-do list. She'd just typed "Chyna Moody" into an Internet search box when her cellphone rang. "Hello, Vivi. How's it going?"

"Hi, Kate." Vivi's voice was bubbling with excitement. "If you have plans tonight, cancel them. We're going out."

"OK." Kate's interest was piqued. "What are we celebrating?"

"Guess who's playing at a club within walking distance of the Hamilton Arms?"

Kate's mind was spinning. Cole was the only musician she knew personally, but his band was under contract with Charley's. "Beats me. Who?"

"Broken Chyna, as in Chyna Moody." Vivi was almost breathless. "We can listen to her music, watch her onstage, and get a handle on what she's like. Maybe we can even talk to her. It'd be safer in a public place too."

"When's her first set?" Kate glanced at her watch. It was just after five o'clock. "And do you think we should ask Cole to go with us? He *does* have a vested interest in talking to her."

"Music starts at nine. You have plenty of time to contact Cole. We can all meet at the hotel and walk to the club. Park in the garage, third floor. That's where my car is. I'll meet you in the lobby at eight."

"That works for me. It's a good thing tomorrow's design review was canceled. Now I don't need to worry about staying out late," Kate said.

"It was canceled? I'm so sorry, Kate." Vivi's voice was tinged with disappointment. "Do you know why?"

"No. I don't even know who called to cancel. She didn't leave her name," Kate said. "I called Jamie Martin and left a message."

"I'm sure it's just some sort of mix-up." Vivi's voice returned to its normal perkiness. "On the plus side, it gives you plenty of time to go out tonight. I'll see you at the Hamilton Arms."

Kate was relieved to have something to take her mind off the phantom phone message. "Sounds good. I'll call Cole and text you whether or not he can go. Bye for now."

After calling Cole, Kate spent the next hour researching Chyna Moody and Broken Chyna. The band had a website and social media page. Chyna had a personal social media account, but the public was only allowed to see photos.

Band members had nicknames like "Menace," "Moocher," and "Maim." Chyna was just "Chyna." All sported several tattoos, ranging from the dagger and blood drops on Menace's arm to the black roses encircling Chyna's neck.

The band's website listed a respectable number of appear-ances throughout Texas, Louisiana, Arkansas, and Mississippi with positive fan comments for each one. Photos showed band members dressed in black, although the drummer was usually shirtless. Chyna's costumes were outrageous. In some pictures they were flashy and revealing; in others she wore Goth outfits.

As wild as they looked, Kate didn't find any newspaper articles about arrests, drug abuse, or violence, although one blogger commented on the destruction of a hotel room. A tough bunch for sure, but nothing pointed to murder.

Kate closed her laptop. It was almost time to see Broken Chyna in person.

Cole strode through the hotel lobby dressed for an evening of rock music.

"Ooh-la-la. Would you look at that, Kate?" Vivi let out a soft catcall. "Not bad for an old man."

Kate cut her eyes to Vivi. "Watch out how you define old," she said, laughing. "He's not much older than I am." Watching Cole approach them in black jeans, a red-and-black Red Hot Chili Peppers T-shirt, and boots, Kate had to agree with Vivi's catcall. He was casually gorgeous.

They made a motley crew walking the two blocks to the rock club—Vivi in her Western shirt, jeans, and boots, and Kate wearing blue jeans and the glittery silver chiffon T-shirt Vanessa had given her for Mother's Day. She'd chosen to wear it to the club because Vanessa said it made her look younger. Kate had a feeling they'd be the oldest people in the joint.

The night was cool and breezy, and Kate was enjoying the walk. "What's this place called?"

"The Edge," Vivi said, adjusting the cuff on her shirt as she walked. "It's dark, loud, and always crowded. They seem to book good bands, if you like that sort of music."

Kate wrinkled her nose. "I don't think this is the type of place any of us would hang out if we weren't on a mission."

"True," said Cole, "although I've spent pretty much all of my life in clubs." He rubbed the tips of his fingers over his T-shirt. "But jazz has always been my genre."

The Edge was located in the bottom floor of an old gray bank building perched near the edge of a narrow sidewalk. "First Southern Bank" was still etched above the doorway, and Kate wondered why the owners didn't call it The Vault or The Green Stuff. *They must make plenty of it,* she thought, as the line to enter stretched across two other storefronts. "Either The Edge is the place to be, or Chyna's band has a huge following."

"Both, I think." Vivi scanned the crowd. "There's actually a decent mix of ages here."

"Good," said Kate. "Maybe Cole and I won't stand out too much."

They stood in line for twenty minutes. Vivi spent the time talking to people and asking them what they liked about Chyna's music. The general consensus was that her music was gritty and original, her demeanor tough and sassy. Kate was sure they were in for an interesting evening whether or not they were able to talk to the singer.

They paid for the tickets, had their hands stamped at the door, and entered into a world Kate had never experienced. They inched their way through the crowd in search of a place to sit. They were passing by the long, purple back-lit bar when a hand shot out of the crowd and pulled Vivi's sleeve.

Vivi turned and threw her arms around the neck of the tall redhead dressed in leather. Their words were drowned out by the noise of the crowd, but Vivi's head was bobbing up and down. She stepped back and tugged on Kate's arm and yelled, "Follow me." Kate relayed the message and grasped Cole's hand as the three of them followed the redhead through the crowd to a reserved table near the dance floor with a view of the darkened, raised stage behind it.

Vivi's redheaded friend moved closer to Kate. "I hope this table works for you. Enjoy the show."

"Thank you." Kate shouted above the noise. The woman nodded and disappeared in the crowd.

"How did you do that?" Kate said, leaning into her friend's ear.

Vivi grinned. "That was the manager, Pamela Rhys. We worked for the same event planner early in our careers. I've introduced her to some great bands and vice versa. I called her today after I called you. I'll tell you what she said about Chyna after the show. I wanted the table to be a surprise."

"It was." Kate turned to Cole and explained Vivi's working relationship with Pamela Rhys.

To Kate's surprise, Pamela sent over a round of drinks on the house. As soon as the server placed the glasses on the table, the stage lights came on, bathing the room in blue, green, and violet light. The drum-pounding solo opened the show; soon rock guitars joined in, blasting the audience. When it all reached a crescendo of angst, the instrumentation backed off and Chyna's clear, haunting voice took command, reminding Kate of Avril Lavigne, one of Vanessa's favorite singers. Kate stole a look at Cole, who seemed mesmerized by the singer. "What do you think?" she asked.

He didn't take his eyes off the porcelain-skinned singer

with waist-length, jet-black hair and a tattooed vine of roses, matching the design on her neck, twisting down the inside of her microphone arm. "She's good. Very good."

Chyna held out the last note of the song so long that Kate was waiting for the woman to collapse from the effort. When the note ended, the percussionist tapped a light beat. The singer switched the microphone to her other hand and lifted the tattooed arm over her head. "Hello, Fort Worth! We're Broken Chyna." Chyna proceeded to introduce the members of her band in a voice not as smooth as her singing.

She bent over from the waist, letting her hair fall to the floor before standing up and sending it cascading behind her back. "We're gonna play a few original songs. That OK with you?"

The crowd erupted, and the band launched into a five-song set. About fifteen seconds into the third song, Kate caught her breath. The notes were hauntingly familiar. When Chyna sang the first line, Kate knew it was the same song Brice Denman claimed as his on his video. She turned and looked at Cole, his eyes still glued on the singer. He was probably asking himself the same question Kate had. *Did Brice or Chyna write the song?*

Near the end of the last number, the server appeared to refill their drinks. Cole scribbled a note asking to see Chyna during the break and asked the server to pass it along to her.

Cole leaned toward Kate. "Hopefully the note will get us a visit with Chyna."

Kate was relieved when the music faded after the last song in the set. Her ears were ready for a break, and she was anxious to meet Chyna. All eyes at the table were glued to the side of the stage as Chyna stepped down. The server held the note out to her and pointed at Cole. The singer's eyes drifted to the table and widened as they fell on Cole. She shook her head and ran backstage.

"Looks like you've lost your touch," Kate joked, bumping her shoulder against Cole's arm.

"As long as you don't run away, I'll survive." Cole grinned. "I wonder what set her off."

"I don't know," Vivi said, her eyes focusing behind Cole. "But I think we're about to find out."

A giant of a man seemed to appear out of nowhere. He hauled Cole up by his shirt collar. "You gotta leave now." He scowled at Vivi and Kate. "You too. And all of you are banned from the club for good. Got it?"

Two other beefy club employees stood close by to increase the intimidation. Kate didn't see Vivi's friend, Pamela. Kate and Vivi stood up and followed the bouncer, who was still holding onto Cole's shirt. When they were outside the door, Vivi whirled around to face the muscled man. "What did we do to deserve being kicked out of the club?"

"It don't matter. You gotta leave. Don't come back." He stood with his arms folded while the trio walked down the block. He was still watching them when Kate stopped at the corner and looked back at him.

Vivi pulled out her cellphone. "I'm calling Pamela to find out what's going on here." After a few seconds, she returned the phone to her purse. "She didn't pick up. I guess the show must go on."

"So, what did Pamela say about Chyna and her reputation?" Kate rubbed her ears. "My ears are still ringing."

"When I called about reserving a table for tonight, I asked her about the band. She said they have a large following in this area and they bring in new customers each time they perform," Vivi said. "But Chyna has a temper, and sometimes they break equipment and furniture at some venues. Not here, though."

"Maybe Brice was a victim of that temper." Cole started walking. "We have to find a way to talk to her, temper or not."

"We just go back to Plan A," Kate said, entering the parking garage. "Go to her apartment."

They were halfway to the elevator when two masked men emerged from the shadows and ran toward them screaming. The tallest one punched Cole in the stomach, knocking him to the ground. He stuck his booted foot on Cole's shoulder. "Be careful of the company you keep."

Kate screamed, and the other man grabbed her with one arm and pressed a knife into her side. "Shut up!"

She cut her eyes to Vivi and stood still.

Feeling the blade through her shirt, Kate thought about the Mace on her keychain. If she could slip her hand into her pocket and grab it, would she be able to spray the attacker's eyes without getting Mace into her own?

Her thoughts were interrupted when a sedan entered the garage. The startled attacker relaxed his grip and Vivi sprang into action, landing a kick to his knife arm that caused him to drop the weapon. Vivi then swiped her foot to knock the knife out of range.

"I suggest you leave. Now," she said, her voice loud and controlled.

The masked man flung Kate to the ground and both of them ran for cover behind a concrete pillar. "Who'da thought the short one would be a ninja or somethin'?" asked the one man as they bolted from the garage.

Kate was sprawled on the parking lot. "Kate, are you all right?" Vivi ran to her friend.

"I'm OK. My hands are a little scraped." Kate reached up to take Vivi's outstretched hand and scrambled to her feet.

Cole sat up, rubbed his shoulder where the attacker's

boot had been, and struggled to stand. He stood dazed for a moment before taking a step.

He walked to the entrance of the parking garage and came loping back to them. "I wanted to make sure they were gone. Let's get on the elevator." He put his arm around Kate. "Are you sure you're all right?"

Kate nodded. "Shaken, but unhurt except for a few scrapes." She looked at Vivi. "Where did you learn those moves?"

"I took self-defense classes when I was younger," she answered. "My mom thought it was a good idea to be able to protect myself."

"Very impressive." Kate managed a slight smile. "I'm glad you took those classes."

"Me too," Cole added. "Thanks for the save."

The elevator was waiting on the first floor. The doors opened as soon as Cole pushed the button, and they boarded quickly.

"Cole, what do you think that was all about?" Kate rubbed her palms on her jeans to brush off the dirt.

"Don't know." He was quiet until the doors opened on the third floor. "Chyna probably saw my photo on the news and feared for her life."

Vivi stepped off first. "We should call the police."

"I don't think so." Cole's eyes drifted from Vivi to Kate. "Your friend Peter would only look for a way to blame me."

He sounded unnaturally calm, remote even, for a man who'd just been attacked. Kate looked at the handsome man who'd brought so much drama into her life in Texas. Should she be afraid for her own life?

Fifteen

Kate shifted on the soft cushion of her love seat and held a bowl of oatmeal in one hand while operating the TV remote with the other. So far, there'd been nothing on the morning news about Brice Denman or Cole. She was still a little sore from when the attacker had thrown her to the ground the previous night, but she was relieved she hadn't ended up as the subject of a newscast. Had they done the right thing by not calling the police? Vivi had probably been right when she suggested reporting the incident, but Kate had feared it would only bring another lecture from Peter about staying out of the murder investigation.

Her cellphone rang on the cushion beside her. Vivi's name popped up on the caller ID. Kate tossed the remote onto the love seat and picked up the phone. "Good morning, ninja. How's it going?"

"I'm on my way to work, so I thought I'd call and check on you." Vivi sounded cheerful, but concern tinted the edges of her words.

"I'm a bit stiff, but otherwise OK. I'm almost glad my appointment at the Governor's Mansion was postponed or I'd be on the road now too. I'm happy to be taking it easy today." Kate placed her bowl on the coffee table. "Boy, you sure surprised me when you kicked the knife out of the guy's hand. Thanks again."

"I surprised myself. I still practice from time to time, but I haven't taken a refresher class in years. Until now, I never felt the need. Although, I leave events alone late at night. It's nice to know I can protect myself. Not to change the subject, but when are you going to call to reschedule the meeting in Austin?"

Kate shifted her position on the sofa. "I'm not sure. The assistant didn't leave instructions. I'll call Jamie Martin again."

"Good deal. Listen, I have an incoming call to take. Let me know what you find out from Jamie. Bye!" Vivi signed off.

Kate immediately dialed Jamie Martin's number and again reached her voice mail. She asked her to please call with an update about the rescheduled wedding dress design review meeting.

Kate left the television muted while she finished her oatmeal and pondered what to do with her unexpected free time. She'd blocked out the entire day for the trip to Austin. This might be the perfect chance to start the sheer-sleeve, floral-lace shirt to display in Once Upon a Yarn.

But first she wanted to take a long, hot bath to relieve the stiffness in her body. She put her breakfast dishes in the kitchen sink and headed to the bathroom with visions of votive candles and lavender oil floating through her mind.

Relaxed and refreshed, Kate slipped into a cotton sundress and sighed. She felt ready to start on the lace shirt. She was halfway to the studio when her cellphone rang in the living room. Trotting to the coffee table, she grabbed it before the caller could hang up. "Hello?"

"Mrs. Stevens, this is Jamie Martin from Sophia Jackson's office. You're late for the review of designs with Miss Jackson, and she and her mother are quite upset. Are you almost here?"

Kate sank to the sofa. "I ... no, I'm still in Sage Hills," she stammered. "Yesterday afternoon I received a call cancelling the appointment. The person identified herself as someone from your office."

"That's odd. I'm the only one responsible for contacting wedding vendors. Did she give you a name?"

"No." Kate closed her eyes and tried to remember the exact words the caller used. "It was a short message. She didn't leave a phone number. I did call you twice and left messages because yours is the only contact number I have."

"I see." Jamie Martin paused. "I'm sorry, Mrs. Stevens. My phone stopped working, and I have to get it replaced. I didn't receive your messages."

"Miss Martin, I can be in Austin by three thirty this afternoon if Miss Jackson still has time to see me." Kate took a deep breath. "I'd cleared the whole day for her."

"Please hold a moment. I'll see if that works."

Kate's mind went into overdrive while she was on hold. *Who in the world cancelled the appointment?* Was someone trying to undermine Jamie Martin or Carolina or her?

"Mrs. Stevens?" Jamie Martin sounded irritated. "Mrs. Jackson and Miss Carolina would be most appreciative if you could be here at three thirty today. The bride-to-be is anxious to see your designs. I apologize for the inconvenience."

"It's no inconvenience at all. I'll see you at three thirty. Thank you."

"Thank you."

By the time Kate had merged onto I-35 South to Austin, she'd spent nearly an hour listening to Cole's new CD and ruminating on why someone would call and say the appointment had been cancelled. She still had no answer. Hopefully this wouldn't jeopardize her relationship with the bride and her mother. As the CD repeated for the second time, her mind switched to Brice Denman's murder, Chyna's refusal to speak with Cole, and the attack in the parking garage. And Cole and Peter. She wasn't only caught in the middle of a murder investigation, she was torn between her feelings for the two men. She wanted to believe Cole was innocent, but her life had become so chaotic since he'd reentered it. First she'd become consumed with proving his innocence, and now masked men were holding her at knifepoint in parking garages. She also thought of Cole's mobile, unstructured life as a musician. He'd always be chasing a better sound, the next gig, a hit song. She also recognized her own desire for stability. What she wanted most in life was to see Vanessa happy and healthy. She wished to live in a safe, comfortable home, to spend time with people she cared about, and to earn a reasonable living with her God-given talent for crochet design. And one day she'd like to share her safe haven with a man who loved her. *Will that ever be possible with Cole?*

The investigation seemed to have changed Peter. Normally charming in a witty sort of way, lately he'd become more serious and overprotective of her. *But Peter is just doing his job,* she thought. *Just like Cole, Peter is a product of his job. It's just an occupational hazard.* Would they be able to return to their easygoing, comfortable relationship?

As Kate approached Austin, the traffic became more challenging to maneuver, so she traded the CD for the local radio station traffic report. She was glad to have her mind busy with something other than recent frustrations. She laughed when she realized what she was thinking. *Is it possible to be thankful for traffic?*

Before she knew it, Kate was pulling up to the parking garage at Twelfth Street and San Jacinto Boulevard. Pausing before the entrance, she shuddered, remembering the feel of the knife jabbing her in the side at the parking garage the previous night. Maybe she should find a metered parking spot on the street. As soon as the thought flittered through her mind, a horn blasted her back into reality. She was holding up other folks who wanted to get into the garage. Swallowing her fear, she pulled in, stopped to get a ticket at the gate, and found a space close to the elevator. A car filled with a young couple and three children pulled in nearby, so she waited until they had their group organized and walked to the elevator with them.

The Governor's Mansion still impressed her. Remembering the drill from her first visit, Kate went directly to the security screening area at the Colorado and Tenth Street entrance. Jamie Martin again met her in the lobby.

"Mrs. Stevens, thank you so much for coming after such a strange mix-up." She held her hand out, and her eyes drifted to the portfolio under Kate's left arm. "I left instructions for the DPS Troopers to search your portfolio and bag, but to allow you to bring them in with you. I trust it was a smooth process."

"It was, thank you." Kate shifted the portfolio to her other arm. "I'm looking forward to showing the Jacksons my designs."

Jamie smiled. "They're most excited to see them."

Kate followed her to the same parlor they'd met in during her first trip to Austin. Carolina Jackson bubbled over to greet Kate as soon as she walked in the door. "I'm dying to see your designs," she said, eyeing the portfolio. Behind her, Sophia Jackson stood silently beside a tall, elegant woman with high cheekbones, dark eyes, and black hair knotted at the nape of her neck. Kate was sure this was Marisa Sanchez, the designer darling of the rich and powerful. She recognized her from fashion design magazines. Kate hesitated, looking to the first lady for an introduction and clues on how to proceed. But the bride's mother merely smiled briefly and nodded in greeting.

Jamie retreated to an unobtrusive spot in a corner chair. Carolina flounced to the yellow, wood-trimmed sofa and made a show of sitting with affected poise, her skirt nearly blending with the sofa material. Placing the portfolio on the sofa next to Carolina, Kate smiled, crossed to the two women standing by the fireplace, and looked the first lady of Texas in the eye. "It's good to see you again, Mrs. Jackson." She turned to the other woman and held out her hand. "I'm Kate Stevens."

The woman uncrossed her arms and hesitated before barely touching Kate's proffered hand. "Marisa Sanchez."

"It's an honor to meet you." Kate resisted the urge to wipe her hand on her skirt. "I'm a great admirer of your work." She waited for the designer to respond. When she offered a faint smile, Kate joined Carolina on the sofa, picking up the portfolio and handing it to Carolina. "I created eight designs based on the elements you and your mother pointed out from my portfolio and your photographs during our last meeting. Any of them can be tweaked to your preference."

Kate smiled as Carolina quickly flipped past the first three designs heavily influenced by Sophia Jackson's love of the Southern belle style. Carolina took much more time with the variations of the mermaid cut design, flipping pages back and forth to compare them, and pausing to ask an occasional question. "These are gorgeous. How can I possibly choose?"

"There are three more. If you're undecided, don't try to choose until you've finished looking at them all." Kate stole a peek at Sophia Jackson and Marisa Sanchez. "Your mother and Ms. Sanchez might want to weigh in."

Carolina responded by turning the page to the first of the blended designs. She stared at the first sketch and turned her grinning face to Kate. "How'd you do this?"

"I just doodled with both of your ideas until I found the right mix of design elements."

The young woman addressed her mother for the first time. "Mother, I think you'll like this one. Take a look."

"I will when you've finished looking at all of them." Sophia Jackson seemed reluctant to take even a quick peek at the designs.

Carolina was equally impressed with the second blended design. Kate held her breath as the bride turned the last page to see Kate's favorite of the dresses.

"Oh, Mama, I think you're going to like this one!" Suddenly childlike, she jumped up and scampered to her mother and held up the last page. "Look, she included your magnolias and ruffles in the sleek mermaid design I love."

Kate watched Sophia Jackson's face turn from stone to reluctant approval as the woman's eyes took in the magnolia lace pattern spanning the floor-length wedding gown. The mermaid-cut dress featured a plunging neckline softened by a sheer crocheted yoke in a magnolia blossom design and a full lace godet, also with a magnolia-inspired design, at the bottom of the front skirt. It had a sheer, cutout back with a scalloped drop waist and a gathered, very full, long puddle train in back. She'd even worked a few ruffles into the train design.

After the women discussed the design, Kate quietly interjected, "The train can be bustled with a button and loop—lined, if desired."

Carolina lifted pleading eyes to her mother. "This is the dress; I know it. I don't need to look anymore."

Mrs. Jackson looked resigned to her daughter's wishes. "You're sure?"

"Positively." The bride's chin was set.

"Do you have any questions before I take your measurements?" Kate's eyes drifted from daughter to mother to designer.

Sophia Jackson and Marisa Sanchez exchanged a look, but the designer remained silent. Kate took that as a good sign. The Texas first lady cleared her throat. "You must know, of course, to use the finest of materials."

Kate grinned. "I always do."

"Oh, money should be no object." Sophia Jackson lifted her hand toward her assistant. "But I'll leave that to you and Jamie."

Kate nodded. "I'll email an estimate to Ms. Martin after I select the materials. I'll be ordering them through Once Upon a Yarn. May I tell the shop owner, Paige Bryant, the name of my client?"

Sophia Jackson looked to Jamie Martin, who nodded her head, before answering, "Yes, that would be fine. Please ask her to use discretion."

"I will," Kate said, removing a tape measure and notepad from her purse. She asked Carolina to stand. "This shouldn't take long." Kate knew it put clients at ease to chat during this time, so she asked them to recommend places to see in Austin. "I moved to Texas a year ago, and I'm gradually getting to know it. This has given me a great opportunity to learn about Austin."

After a few minutes, Sophia Jackson and Marisa Sanchez joined in the conversation. The first lady suggested taking the historical walking tour of the Capitol and its environs. The designer mentioned several museums, especially the Mexic-Arte Museum and the Texas Music Museum. Most intriguing to Kate was Carolina's idea to visit the HOPE Outdoor Gallery.

Kate continued taking the young woman's measurements while she waxed poetic about the outdoor gallery.

"It's a community art project with large-scale murals in a three-story area. It's awesome." Her eyes lit up. "It's in the top ten tourist draws in Austin. Some people call it a paint park. I wrote a paper about it in college."

Kate had read online that Carolina had graduated from New York University with a Bachelor of Fine Arts degree in Art.

When Kate tucked her pad, pencil, and measuring tape back into her bag, she had several ideas for sightseeing as well as Carolina's measurements. "Thank you for giving me so many great recommendations." She turned to Carolina. "I think I'll bring some sensible shoes to the next fitting and stop by the outdoor gallery on the way home. I'm always looking for design inspiration."

Carolina spontaneously wrapped her arms around Kate. "I really appreciate everything you're doing for me."

Kate, taken aback by the hug, left with a warmth that was quickly melting the icy reception she had received.

Sixteen

"Broken Chyna can't be doing too well if this is where Chyna lives." Kate pulled to the curb in front of the tiny ramshackle house indicated by her GPS and raised her eyebrows. "The property appraiser's website said this place was built in 1947. Looks like it hasn't been repaired or painted very often since then."

Vivi held up her smartphone. "The map shows this area as Pleasant Grove. Sort of a misnomer, don't you think? I see no groves here."

"Me neither." Kate noticed the peeling paint, loose roof shingles, and overgrown weeds and hedges. "If Chyna was banking on the song Brice poached to make her enough money to get out of this place, it could have pushed her to murder him."

"Yep." Vivi pocketed her phone and opened her door. "Especially if she has illusions of grandeur."

They stood on the curb and studied the house. "It should be a crime to paint a house swimming-pool blue," said Vivi, shaking her head. "The entire house."

"The band's website listed a lengthy tour schedule, so maybe she's not here a lot." Kate couldn't imagine living in that house alone. "I wonder if she has a roommate."

"I guess we'll find out." Vivi led the way up the cracked driveway to the house.

Kate pushed the old doorbell and listened for a chime. Nothing. She tried the screen door and found it unlocked, so she eased it open and rapped three times.

A door slammed at the house next door and an elderly woman with light pink hair walked across her lawn toward them. "You looking for Evelyn?"

"No, ma'am," said Vivi. "We're here to see Chyna. Are we at the right house?"

"You sure are, but Evelyn—she's Chyna's grandmother—has been in the nursing home since she fell three weeks ago. Chyna always visits her every Friday morning when she's in town. I'll bet that's where she is."

Kate made a concentrated effort to not stare at the woman's botched dye job. "Do you know which nursing home?"

The woman squeezed her eyes shut in concentration, shook her head, and opened them. "I can't remember. So sorry, but my mind's not so good these days. But I imagine she'll be back after a while. As far as I know, she's in town for the next couple of weeks. Chyna always lets me know when she'll be gone so I can watch the place."

"Thank you. You've been very helpful. What's your name?" The kind woman reminded Kate of her own grandmother, who had died many years ago.

The woman tittered and waved a hand through the air. "Oh, where are my manners? I'm Pat … Pat Renshaw. I'm pleased to meet you." She glanced at the road as an older-model Chevrolet pulled up in front of her house. "I have to go now. That's my friend Sally. She's here to take me to bingo at the senior center."

"Thank you, Miss Pat. We appreciate your help," Vivi said. "Have fun at bingo."

Kate and Vivi watched the woman take measured steps toward the white sedan waiting for her.

"I hope I'm half as cool as that woman when I'm her age." Vivi chuckled. "Maybe I'll even go for the pink hair."

"You could pull off any color hair you want." Kate started walking to the car, and Vivi fell into step beside her. "So, what are the odds Chyna is really at a nursing home visiting an infirm grandmother?"

"Pat seemed sincere enough," Kate said with a shrug, "but who knows if Chyna told her the truth."

Kate started the van and turned on the air conditioning as soon as they were in the car. "Thank goodness for AC." She ran the back of her hand across her forehead. "Do you want to wait here and see if Chyna comes home?"

"I wonder if there's anyplace to eat around here." Vivi patted her stomach. "My tummy is growling."

"It wouldn't hurt to drive around a bit and see. Do a search on your cellphone and see if you find anything." Kate caught a movement out of the corner of her eye and whipped her head around to get a better look at Chyna's house. "No way! Is that Cole walking around the house?"

"You'd know better than I, my friend," Vivi teased as she turned to look out the window. "Yep, your Cole radar is working. I don't suppose we could get away with slinking down in our seats."

"We could," replied Kate, "if we were in your car."

Vivi chuckled, but her smile soon disappeared. "Why do you suppose Cole is here by himself? He wasn't at the music store when Dexter gave us the address."

Kate's heart pounded against her chest. "Is it possible Cole knew Chyna before Brice was killed?"

"Kate, could Cole be guilty? I mean, how well do you really know him?"

Before Kate could answer, Cole turned and walked across the lawn toward them. Vivi tapped Kate's arm and pointed to the Mace can dangling on the key chain hanging from the ignition. "That's not going to help us on the key ring, so be prepared to hit the gas pedal if he tries anything."

Kate gripped the steering wheel harder. "I hope that's not necessary."

"Me too," Vivi replied.

Cole rapped on the driver's-side window with his knuckles. Kate looked up at his face and was startled by the look in his eyes. She truly wondered if Cole could be the killer.

She rolled down the window. "What are you doing here?"

"I might ask you the same thing." He didn't sound irritated or angry. Just surprised.

Kate pulled her sunglasses down her nose a bit and looked at him over the lenses. "Are you sure there's not any connection between you and Chyna? She did act strange when you asked to meet with her."

Cole glared at her and slammed his fist hard on the door of the van. "I can't believe you'd think that, much less ask it." His nostrils flared. "Has Peter Matthews gotten to you?"

She winced. "We gotta go now." Kate pressed the button to close the window, put the van in gear, and pulled away from the curb before Cole could react. She drove silently until she reached the stop sign at the end of the street. "I won't let anyone talk to me that way anymore."

Vivi leaned over and placed a hand on Kate's shoulder. "You did great. His reaction was odd, but sometimes people hide their true colors. It takes some time to see them for who they really are."

"True." Kate pressed the accelerator. "It isn't pretty sometimes."

Vivi's eyes softened. "Do you still want to find lunch somewhere and go back to talk to Chyna?"

The question hung in the air while Kate considered it.

"No, I don't think so. I'd like to solve the mystery, but I'm not so sure I'm willing to stick my neck out for a man who speaks to me that way. As hot as it is, I'd rather spend the time in my garden with flowers that grow rather than with someone who could hurt other people."

The dirt felt good under Kate's fingernails. Pulling pesky weeds and rearranging the dirt around the colorful African daisies allowed her to productively release her pent-up stress. Sitting among the flowers in her floppy straw hat filled her with satisfaction. She moved onto the pale pink and yellow lantana, freeing the flowers from the vines creeping around them. Soon she had several piles of weeds along the edge of the garden, which she would bag all at one time.

She'd saved the line of dusty miller plants, which created a frilly border for the garden, to clean out last. Kate loved the whimsical, fine, silver leaves that reminded her of lace. They were dainty works of art, like the lace Kate was creating for Carolina Jackson's wedding dress. She was halfway down the dusty millers when the hairs on the back of her neck prickled, sending a chill through her body despite the heat radiating from the soil.

She didn't see a shadow, and there was no sound. Maybe it was just a feeling, but someone was behind her!

Kate grabbed the three-prong hand rake off the ground and slowly turned, first her head, then her shoulders. She nearly fell over when she twisted around to find Cole standing ten feet behind her, a huge bouquet of gerbera daisies in his hand.

"Cole!" Kate stood, hands gripping the handle of the

cultivator. She glanced down her side yard, trying to determine if Vivi had left for work yet. Kate's cellphone was of no use; she'd left it on the kitchen table.

"Kate, I'm sorry I lost my temper. It's not like me." He held out the flowers. "I'm at my wits' end, and I lost my head. I'm just so tired of being accused of something I could never have done."

Kate stood still and ignored the flowers long enough for Cole to hold them down at his side. "Why were you at Chyna's house today?" she asked.

Cole squinted and wiped perspiration from his forehead. "It's really hot in the sun. Can we go inside?"

Kate wasn't ready to be alone inside with Cole. "I'm really grubby. I'd rather stay out here. But we can sit on the patio in the shade."

"OK." Cole followed her to the patio. They sat across from each other at a small café table she'd picked up at a garage sale shortly after moving to Sage Hills. He placed the flowers on the table, looking exhausted and sad. "Yesterday morning I found out the club owner nullified our contract. Evan tried to smooth over the legalities, but nothing worked. The band is finished here. The guys are leaving tomorrow, but I have to stay. The rest of the tour is on hold indefinitely."

"I'm sorry. I know that must be difficult for you." Kate rubbed a water spot from the table, raised her eyes to Cole, and waited for him to continue.

"After my meeting with Gus and the club manager, I decided I'd have to look for Chyna myself since you were in Austin and Vivi was working. It's the only thing I could think of to do." Cole ran his fingers along the plastic wrap encasing the flowers. "I spent the day trying to find old acquaintances from the university and in the music scene, hoping someone could tell me about her. It took a while, but by the end of the day I'd learned she was living with her grandmother in Pleasant Grove."

"I see." Kate's breathing was returning to normal.

Cole moved the flowers over and reached his hand across the table. She gazed at the fingers that so beautifully manipulated his trumpet. She couldn't see those same fingers wrapped around a gun. She put her hand over his. "You'll get through this."

"But will *we*?" Cole put his other hand over hers and squeezed.

"That, I'm not so sure about." Kate managed a smile. "I guess we'll have to see, won't we? Let's get through the investigation first and see where we are."

"That's fair." He looked at the flowers. "I called Brice's parents yesterday. They didn't know Chyna, but I did learn they're not having a funeral for Brice for a while. They're waiting to have a memorial service after his murder is solved. It's amazing, the power of forgiveness. They don't seem to blame me for Brice's drug addiction or his death. They even offered to call some of his friends and ask about Chyna."

Cole's cellphone rang. He dug it out of his pocket and checked the number. "It's Gus. I need to take this."

Kate picked up the flowers, looked at Cole, and mouthed, "I'll put these in water."

She had one cut glass vase, a garage sale find back in Maine. Deciding to snip the stems and arrange them after Cole left, Kate cut away the plastic wrap with scissors, lowered the bunch into the vase, and set them in the center of the kitchen table next to her cellphone.

Kate looked through the patio door window and saw Cole pacing on the patio, his phone to his ear. She took the opportunity to check her phone for messages and found one from Jamie Martin asking if Kate had chosen the materials for Carolina Jackson's wedding dress yet. The bride was anxious to know.

"It's been less than a day," she muttered. "They tell me I'm good, but I'm not *that* good."

After checking her calendar to make sure she didn't have any appointments for the next day, Kate sent Jamie a text saying she'd spend the next day in the city searching for the perfect materials, and to please reassure Carolina that the dress would be ready in plenty of time for the wedding.

Jamie's reply was almost immediate. "Thank you so much. I'll pass that along to Miss Carolina."

Kate sighed. She'd be going into Fort Worth tomorrow.

Cole tapped on the patio door and stuck his head inside. "Gus needs me back at the hotel. I have to go. I'll call you tomorrow, OK?"

Kate stepped to the door and opened it wider. "Sounds good. I'll be out scouting for wedding dress material tomorrow, so there's no telling where you'll find me."

He gave her a quick peck on the cheek and stepped back before she could react. "I'm glad we talked. I feel better."

"Me too." Kate smiled. "Thank you for the flowers. They're lovely."

Kate closed the door and leaned back against it, closing her eyes. She couldn't remember a time when she'd been more confused.

Seventeen

"Kate, I didn't think you'd ever get here this morning!" Paige almost speed-walked through Once Upon a Yarn to greet her as soon as she walked through the door. It was nearing eleven o'clock. "I've been dying to know the identity of your client and which dress she chose ever since you called yesterday."

"I wasn't trying to torture you by making you wait, but I figured you'd enjoy hearing the entire story." Kate grinned. She was happy to be spending much of the day in this needlecraft heaven. "I was given permission to disclose her identity, but I was told to ask for your discretion."

"Of course." Paige's eyes sparkled with anticipation.

"It is none other than Carolina Jackson, the daughter of Governor Colt Jackson!"

Paige squealed and threw her arms around Kate's neck. "Wow! How about a cup of tea while you tell me everything? Then we can get to work selecting everything you need for the dress."

Kate followed Paige to the cozy sitting area and opened her portfolio on the table. "Which one do you think Carolina chose?"

"My guess, it wasn't one of the Southern belle–type gowns," said Paige, leaving the tea to steep in the dainty china cups while she perused color photocopies of Kate's dress designs. "I'll bet it was the magnolia dress. It is stunning."

"That's the one, and her mother likes it too." Kate flipped to the dress in question. "I'm glad. I'm so looking forward to making this dress."

Kate melted into the sofa. It felt good to escape the

murder drama and talk shop with Paige. She described her second trip to the Governor's Mansion. When she mentioned Marisa Sanchez, Paige jumped up. "Stop right there! I'm going to get our tea now so I won't need to get up during this part of the story."

Paige returned and placed two cup-and-saucer sets on the table. "So Marisa Sanchez was there when you arrived? Must have been interesting."

"To say the least." Kate smiled, remembering her struggle to maintain her composure around the successful designer. "I concentrated on Carolina. She loved all of the designs, but her reaction to the magnolia dress was priceless. So was her mother's. I surprised them."

Kate and Paige chatted about the experience until they finished their tea. Then they began searching for the materials for Carolina's dress. They browsed a number of Paige's in-store catalogs as well as several online wholesale companies. Occasionally Paige left the sitting area to wait on customers, but by midafternoon, they'd selected and ordered everything needed to create Carolina Jackson's dream wedding dress.

"This was just what I needed," Kate said, collecting her designs, copies of order forms, and catalogs Paige had given her, before settling back on the sofa. "There's nothing like discussing a challenging design project with a friend to distract you from life's curveballs."

Paige took off her reading glasses and let them dangle from the chain around her neck. "I take it you mean the murder involving your musician friend. It was all over the news for a few days, but I've not seen anything for a while."

"Yes, it's been very distracting."

"Anything new on that front?"

"I wish," Kate said. "Peter keeps calling Cole the main

suspect, but they haven't arrested him yet. It's wearing on Cole and, to be honest, on our friendship."

"So, the client of your career contacted you at the perfect time. The dress will give you something positive to focus on and keep your mind off murder."

"I'm blessed indeed." Kate looked at her watch and stood up. "I'd best get going if I want to beat rush hour. I'm afraid I've filled your entire day."

"Nonsense. This has been fun." Paige gave Kate a quick hug. "I appreciate you. There are bigger, fancier shops than mine, but you chose to purchase supplies here. It means a lot to me."

Kate walked to the front door with Paige beside her. "I'll be back when my order arrives, if not before."

"When do you go back to Austin?"

"Next week. I'll be pinning the muslin mock-up. I'll keep you posted." Kate pushed on the door. "Thanks for everything."

Kate stepped into the late-afternoon sunshine feeling more relaxed than she had since Vanessa first spotted Cole's photo outside of Charley's Jazz Room two weeks ago yesterday. Designing Carolina Jackson's wedding dress could take her career to a whole new level, and Kate was now confident she could handle it.

Before she pulled out of the parking lot, Kate turned on the local oldies radio station, turned up the volume, and sang along with every song between Once Upon a Yarn and Hawkins Drive in Sage Hills.

Her singing stopped when she turned onto Hawkins Drive and found a fire truck, ambulance, and police car outside her home. Kate's heart began racing as she tried to make sense of the scene. *What now?*

A fireman was hosing down a smoldering fire on her lawn. Officer Johnny Castille was on her front porch, examining the open front door. Kate pulled the van into Vivi's driveway and parked, knowing her friend was working late. She watched as water stopped flowing from the hose. The fireman placed it on the ground and examined the burnt spot. A man who'd just arrived in the Fire Services SUV walked up to him.

Peter pulled up in his Taurus as Kate crossed the road. She strode directly to his car and waited for him to open his door. "Peter, what in the world is going on?"

"You'd know if you'd answer your phone when I tried to call." Peter's voice was mixed with concern and frustration. "Are you avoiding me?"

"Not at all. I had my radio turned up on my way back from Fort Worth. I guess I didn't hear it ring." She pointed to the man who was talking to the firefighter. "Who's that?"

"Bud Steen, the fire inspector. He's a good guy." Peter motioned for her to follow him. "Let's get some answers. All I know is Johnny called me and said he'd been dispatched to your house for a possible arson and burglary."

The fire inspector met Kate and Peter halfway up the driveway. "What can you tell us?" Peter asked after introducing Kate to Bud Steen.

"Not much at this point. We don't know what exactly was burned here, but there seem to be bits of charred paper in the area. We'll know more after we run some tests." Steen glanced at the cottage and back to Peter. "Have you been inside?"

Peter shook his head. "No. I just got here." He looked at Kate. "I'm going to finish the walk-through with Johnny and Bud. Once the building is cleared, we'll go through the house with you to see if anything is missing."

Several neighbors were congregated in the street, including the eccentric Frieda Mahl, who believed in the power of burning sage, using crystals, and wearing amulets. Not much escaped Frieda. She kept an eye on all of the houses in the neighborhood. "Peter, I want to speak to my neighbors while you're inside," Kate said. "They might be worried about me. I want to let them know I'm fine."

His eyes drifted to the small circle of residents whose attention was riveted on Kate's house. "It's all right, but don't give them any information. Tell them everything is fine except the burnt patch in your yard." Peter turned and hurried up to the house.

Kate joined her neighbors in the street and did her best to be calm, cool, and collected. "Thank you for checking on me. I was in Fort Worth when the fire started, so I'm fine."

Frieda, her fluffy white hair nearly reaching her waist, was hovering on the edge of the group as if waiting for something. Because she lived two doors down and was constantly watching, Kate was anxious to talk to her. Maybe she'd seen the person who set the fire. Kate broke away from the other neighbors and approached the old woman, who seemed to be talking to the air. "Frieda, I'm so glad you're here. Did you see anyone around my house this afternoon while I was away?"

The woman whirled around, her hair whipping like a cyclone. When she stopped, she reached out with bony fingers and grabbed Kate's arm, pressing an object into her hand and gazing at her with blazing eyes. "Protect yourself from danger, child. Keep this with you. You hear?" She released Kate's arm and flittered to her own yard, dancing among the blue gazing ball, birdbaths, and flower beds.

Kate opened her hand to see a wooden carved Celtic cross,

long considered a symbol of protection. Kate considered the emergency vehicles in front of her home and the burnt patch smoldering in her yard. Obviously she needed protection from something. But what? She would have preferred information to the gift, but it was thoughtful of Frieda.

Officer Castille strode down the driveway. "Mrs. Stevens, would you walk through the house with us to see if anything is missing?"

"Sure." She cast one last peek at Frieda, who was still moving up the walkway among her lawn ornaments.

"The house wasn't ransacked. It seems like they were looking for something in particular, found it quickly, and took it out front to destroy it in some sort of display of power or intimidation." He ushered her through the front door into the living room, where Peter was waiting. "Any idea who would want to intimidate you?"

Kate thought of her unofficial investigation into Brice Denman's murder. The attack in the parking garage was scary, and now this. "Peter, there's something I need to tell you."

He looked at her sharply. "Yes?"

Kate told Peter and Johnny about the incident after visiting The Edge. "Cole and Vivi were with me to see Broken Chyna perform. We were having a night out."

Peter arched an eyebrow. "A night on the town? That doesn't sound like you."

"I'm getting more adventurous, I guess." Kate wanted to change the subject. She turned to Officer Castille. "Where do you want to me to start?"

"Let's start here and work our way through." He stepped out of her way. "Look around and tell us if there's anything out of place."

Her living room furnishings were sparse, her decor simple.

Nothing was out of place. The kitchen was fine, as was the bathroom. In the bedroom, Kate stopped in front of her closet. "Did you go in my closet when you searched earlier? I always keep it closed."

"Yes, ma'am. To make sure no intruders were hiding in there. But it was opened just like that when I walked in." Officer Castille swept the room with his eyes. "Anything else out of order?"

"Not that I can tell," Kate said. They stepped into the hall and entered Kate's studio. Right away she noticed what was missing—the sketches of the bridal gown designs she'd created for Carolina Jackson. "My designs are gone." Peter and Officer Castille exchanged a silent look, which didn't go unnoticed by Kate. "What is it?"

Peter bobbed his chin. Although the senior police officer in rank and experience, Peter had no jurisdiction in Sage Hills. He was deferring to Johnny. The younger officer hesitated. "It's too soon to tell, but there's a chance your designs were what was set on fire outside."

"I'm getting a curious sense of déjà vu," Peter said, referring to the incident earlier in the year when a sociopath moved in next door and took her designs as a way to scare her into his arms.

"Yes, it does bring back memories." Kate grinned. "But this time it's different."

Peter cocked his head. "How so?"

"This time the originals are safely locked in a safe deposit box at the bank, so if those are sketches burning on the lawn, they're only copies I scanned and printed from the computer." Kate laughed at the look on Peter's face.

"The longer you live in Texas, the shrewder you get," Peter said, admiration flickering on his face before fading into serious concern. "But this very well could be tied to Brice Denman and Cole. Stay away from Cole. All this could be designed by the perp to distract you from finding the truth about Brice Denman's murder."

"I'm doing fine," Kate replied. "You worry too much."

"I'm a cop—and your friend," Peter said, holding her gaze with his eyes. "It's what I do. I'd feel better if you'd leave the investigating to professionals and focus on what you do best."

Kate pulled her eyes away and walked Johnny Castille and Peter to the front door. She watched them cross her lawn to the fire inspector. They stood facing the burnt patch of grass, their backs to her. A minute later, Inspector Steen turned around and sauntered toward her. "Mrs. Stevens, the fire is out, so I'm dismissing the fire crew." He handed her his business card. "My office will be making a thorough investigation. If you have any questions or think of anything that might be helpful, please don't hesitate to call."

She took the card. "I'll keep that in mind. Thank you."

Inspector Steen walked to the street where Peter and Officer Castille were standing between their cars. Kate stood on her porch and watched them drive away before she retraced their steps to the scorched piece of lawn. Frieda's words played in her head. *Protect yourself from danger, child. Keep this with you.* Kate fished the small carved cross from her pocket and rubbed her fingers across the Celtic knots etched in the wood. Although it was a beautiful piece of art, she didn't believe in trusting manmade objects for protection. But she had faith in God.

She also trusted Peter to do what he thought was right. Yet she questioned his objectivity concerning Cole. *Stay away from Cole. All this could be designed by the perp to distract you from finding the truth about Brice Denman's murder.* Was he doing everything he could to determine who really killed Brice Denman? Or could he be right—was Cole the one who pulled the trigger on his old bandmate? If so, why hadn't he been arrested?

Eighteen

When Jamie Martin ushered Kate into the parlor at the Governor's Mansion the following Wednesday morning, the bride was the only person waiting for her. Kate guessed this was for privacy, as she'd be pinning the muslin mock-up dress on her.

Carolina jumped up when Kate walked into the room. "Kate!" She suddenly seemed flustered. "May I call you Kate?"

"Of course." Kate set her workbag on the floor next to the sofa and sat down. "Let's chat a little before we get started."

Kate explained why she was creating a muslin mock-up of Carolina's dress and how it would help as she began crocheting the pieces of the actual gown. The bride listened intently. "Do you have any questions?" Kate asked finally.

Carolina shook her head, so Kate continued. "I'll piece the mock dress together by pinning each piece to conform to your body. Later, I'll stitch it together and use it to make sure each part of your gown is exactly the right size." Her eyes drifted to the ceiling-to-floor windows across the room. The heavy drapes were tied back and sheers covered most of the opening. "Your dress is lined, so there's no need to piece this around a petticoat. Are you comfortable with doing this in front of sheer curtains?"

The bride-to-be nodded. "It's fine."

Kate turned her head to Jamie, who was sitting in a chair on the far side of the room and appeared to be engrossed in paperwork spread out on her lap. Then she returned her attention to Carolina. "Let's work in this corner. The light is perfect." It also provided some privacy, should prying eyes try to see in—but Kate kept that to herself.

She lined up a few essentials on the small corner table beside her—a pincushion, extra pins, tailor's chalk, and the stack of cut fabric pieces.

She worked quickly but with care, asking Carolina general questions about her wedding plans as she pinned pieces of fabric together. Conversation made Kate feel less awkward, and she enjoyed hearing Carolina talk about her big day with excitement. The youngest of three daughters, Carolina was smart, independent, and a little spoiled, but much more pleasant without her mother in the room.

When Kate used up her list of questions, Carolina took over. "So, Kate, are you married?"

Kate inserted several pins in the panels along Carolina's back. "I was for quite a while. He was my high-school sweetheart. We divorced a few years ago."

"Kids?"

"One, my daughter Vanessa. She'll soon be starting her sophomore year at Regency College." Kate liked it better when she was asking the questions. "I'm very proud of her."

Kate finished pinning the material and stood up to examine her work. When she walked around to face Carolina, she found the young woman staring at her.

"I'll bet you tell her, don't you? That you're proud of her, I mean." Carolina's hazel eyes were filled with unspoken emotion.

"Yes, I do." Kate restrained an urge to hug the girl who seemed to need to hear those words from her own mother. Here was a girl with a life most would envy, but she didn't feel her mother's pride and acceptance. She took a few steps back from Carolina and asked her to slowly turn around so she could check her handiwork. "Everything looks good. Hold your arms up, and I'll pull it over your head."

Carolina raised her arms, and Kate eased the muslin over the young woman's head without turning the garment inside out.

Kate turned her back and faced Jamie as Carolina slipped back into her sundress. The first lady's assistant was engrossed in sending a text message. "Excuse me, Jamie." Kate waited for her to lift her head. "I'm about finished here. Does Mrs. Jackson wish to see me before I leave?"

Jamie shook her head. "Mrs. Jackson has another appointment."

Kate folded the material, making sure the pins didn't shift, and slid the mock dress into her bag. "By the way, Miss Jackson, thanks for telling me about the HOPE Outdoor Gallery. I researched it online and was so enthralled that I brought a pair of sneakers with me so I can stop by there on the way home."

"You're welcome, and please call me Carolina." The bride smiled. "Make sure you pick up a bottle of water on your way there. It'll be hot on the concrete. I hope you enjoy the Foundation. That's what the locals call it. I'd like to know what you think."

"I'll do all of the above. I actually have a small cooler with bottled water in my car," said Kate. "Thank you, Carolina."

Kate collected the rest of her supplies and tucked them into the side pocket of her bag. "Jamie, I'll email you when the gown is ready for a first fitting."

Kate was enthralled by the three levels of concrete canvases exploding with color at the HOPE Outdoor Gallery. She'd exchanged her sandals for sneakers and locked her purse in the van, so she carried only her water bottle as she walked through the maze of bright walls and ledges.

The Foundation had been created from an abandoned construction site intended to be condominiums. The outdoor gallery was now a bustling hub for street art in the city. The images were large and bold and as diverse as the artists who painted them. There were renderings of African tribal masks, red giant tennis shoes, a blue owl, a psychedelic fish, and the word *love* in a style reminiscent of the 1960s hippie era.

Kate carefully stepped around pieces of wrought iron sticking out of the ground and uneven patches of grass growing between the levels as she made her way up the site. Every so often, she'd press the cool water bottle against her face and neck to cool off. She was thankful she'd remembered to apply sunscreen to her face, arms, and legs. She was enjoying watching the artists at work and listening to visitors of all ages comment on the murals. The creative energy of this place was exactly what she needed. After the excitement of the fire, Kate had avoided contact with both Peter and Cole, partly to have some peace and partly to work on Carolina's dress and other work commitments. The solitude had done wonders for her frame of mind, and hiking through the outdoor gallery lifted her spirits even more.

A group of tourists flooded the area, drawn to the painted panel of intense shaded eyes peering into space. Kate opted to make her way to the next level, where few people were exploring. She was captivated by a series of color-washed portraits—men and women of all ages, ethnicities, shapes, and sizes—and studied the details in them. The world slipped away as she admired the work of unknown but talented artists.

She was ripped from her concentration when her right hand was wrenched behind her and pulled back so far she feared her wrist would break. The attacker's breath reeked of tobacco and was hot on her neck. "You should stay out of other people's business and stay in your own little world." Kate's mind whirled. The water bottle in her left hand was useless, so she let it drop to the ground. "If you scream, I'll really hurt you." He was pulling her to the edge of the concrete tier. He was going to throw her over the side! Kate struggled to think clearly. She eased her hand into the pocket of her sundress and wrapped her fingers around the pepper spray canister Peter had insisted she carry. Pretending to faint, she went limp. As soon as he relaxed his grip a little, she tensed, closed her eyes and sprayed behind her. Too late. Kate was already in the air, tumbling to the ground below her.

Stunned, Kate lay sprawled on the grassy patch as several bystanders hovered around her. She closed her eyes for a moment until a man's voice asked her to open them. "Ma'am, my name is Wayne Powell. I was a medic in the Army. I'll stay with you. Paramedics are already on the way. My wife called them."

Kate's eyes fluttered open. His eyes showed concern, but not fear. She felt safe. "Has anyone ever told you that you look like Denzel Washington?"

He smiled and looked into her eyes before placing his fingers around her left wrist. He was checking her pulse. "Yeah, I get that a lot. Can't act worth a darn, though. What's your name?"

"Kate." She tried to get up but Wayne eased her back onto the ground. "Did he get away? The man?"

He looked up to the level above them as emergency

sirens blasted through the air. "Nope. A group of college guys are holding him." He lifted his head. "Reinforcements have arrived. I'm going to step away from you now, Kate. Everything is going to be OK."

"Thank you, Wayne. I'm glad you were here."

"Me too." Wayne stood up and moved to the edge of the crowd that was forming in the background.

He was replaced by a paramedic who introduced herself as Becky. She took Kate's vital signs, asked her name, and rattled off a series of questions, some relating to how she felt and others seemingly random—the name of the president, the day of the week, and the year.

"You are one lucky lady, Kate Stevens. You didn't break any bones, but you might be sore for a while." Becky tilted her head up at the shadow appearing over them. "I think this police officer would like to speak with you. Are you up to it?"

Kate nodded.

Becky and her partner moved Kate to a stretcher and raised the back so she was sitting up. With efficient speed, Becky put disinfectant on Kate's scraped hands and knees. "Sit here and relax while the officer talks with you. I'll be here if you need me."

The officer introduced himself as Sergio Perez. "I have a few questions for you. I won't keep you long." He looked around at the crowd. "Becky, could we transport Mrs. Stevens to the ambulance for some privacy and shade?"

"Sure." Becky prepared the stretcher as her partner packed up their equipment.

It was a rough ride on the stretcher down a couple of levels to the ambulance, but Kate was relieved to no longer be the center of attention.

She was also glad to get inside the air-conditioned ambulance.

Kate tried to answer each of Officer Perez's questions with brief but accurate answers. She explained she didn't actually see her assailant, so other witnesses would have to identify him.

"Did he say anything to you?"

"Yes, he told me to stay out of other people's business and he'd hurt me if I screamed."

Officer Perez raised his eyebrows. "Why would he say that?"

"I don't know, unless it has something to do with Cole Cutchins, a friend who's a suspect in a Fort Worth murder. We've been trying to find the real killer."

"Investigating officer?"

"Detective Peter Matthews, Fort Worth Police Department." Kate winced. "Do you think what happened today has to do with the murder?"

Officer Perez looked up from his notes. "We'll look into it. Where were you right before you arrived here?

"The Governor's Mansion."

"Taking a tour?"

"No, business." Kate wasn't sure how much to say.

"What kind of business?"

"I'm a crocheter and clothing designer. I'm designing a dress for Carolina Jackson."

His gaze settled on her face. "Who knew you'd be here at the murals today?"

Still addled from the fall, Kate closed her eyes and tried to remember. "Carolina Jackson and Jamie Martin, the first lady's assistant. I told them just before I left the meeting. Miss Jackson is the one who suggested I see it. I can't remember if I mentioned it to anyone at home."

"You've been very helpful." Officer Perez closed his pad. "Thank you for your cooperation."

By the time she'd finished the interview, her attacker had

been taken away in a patrol car, and Kate was feeling more like making the drive home. Officer Perez gave her his business card. "If you think of anything else or have any questions, feel free to call."

"Thank you." Kate looked from the officer to the paramedic. "Am I free to go?"

Officer Perez tilted his chin to Becky. "It's up to her. I'm finished here." He surveyed the surroundings. "Where are you parked?"

"About a block that way," she said, pointing toward the street.

"If you get the green light from the paramedics, I'll walk you to your car."

Kate cast pleading eyes at Becky. "I have quite a drive to Sage Hills. May I go now?"

"Where's Sage Hills?" Becky asked.

"Just west of Fort Worth."

"That *is* a long way." Becky wrapped a blood pressure band around Kate's arm and squeezed the pump. "I just want to check this one more time." Becky paused. "Well, your vitals are OK, but I'd feel better if you'd find a place to stay locally. Is there anyone in Austin you can call?"

Kate shook her head. "I came here on business this morning and stopped by to see this place on my way out of town. I don't know anyone."

Becky's partner materialized with papers for Kate to sign. As soon as she scribbled her signature, he disappeared again.

Becky helped Kate ease off the stretcher. "I want to stick around and see you walk a little before we head out."

When she passed the walking test, Becky gave the OK for Kate to leave. "If you have any visual disturbances or trouble breathing, pull off the road and dial 911. Please be careful."

Officer Perez escorted Kate to her car. "I'm starting to get used to having police officers around," she said, laughing.

Officer Perez stopped walking. "How so?"

What a silly thing to say. Now what's he going to think?

Kate gave the officer an abbreviated version of the fire in her front yard.

"Why didn't you tell me this before?"

"I didn't think it was relevant."

"It could be." He removed a pad from his pocket and scratched some notes. "Sage Hills PD work the incident?"

"Yes. And Detective Matthews was there too. He's a friend."

"I'll check into it. A detective may follow up with you."

They approached Kate's van and she pointed the key fob, unlocking it. "Thanks for the escort."

"You're welcome. Remember the paramedic's instructions." He watched her open the door. "Be careful on the road."

Kate's muscles were stiff by the time she pulled into her driveway and her brain was tired from replaying the last words of her conversation with Officer Perez for three hours. Was it possible that whoever was trying to scare her away from the investigation had followed her to Austin? She turned off the ignition and grabbed her purse and canvas bag before unlocking the car door. Her entire body ached as she pushed the door open and slid her feet onto the concrete. Standing up, she found herself face-to-face with Peter.

"I don't know whether to hug you or lock you up for safe keeping." He grabbed her by the shoulders and looked down at her. "Why don't you answer your phone?"

Kate bit her lip. "I had the ringer on silent when I went to the Governor's Mansion this morning. I forgot to turn it back on when I went to the HOPE Outdoor Gallery. It's been a tiring afternoon. Why are you here?"

"I heard about your tumble from the wall. Officer Perez contacted me to verify your story about the Denman murder and the fire in your yard. I tried to call. Several times. It was either send out an APB or sit on your doorstep until you arrived." Peter took her arm and led her to the front door. "I thought you'd prefer this. Plus, I have something to tell you."

Kate froze. "What is it?"

"Let's go inside." He took her keys from her hand and unlocked the door.

"No, tell me now." She dreaded his answer.

"OK." He turned to face her. "First, Officer Perez said the Austin PD is taking an interest in your case because you're connected with the Governor's Mansion and an active murder investigation. That's a good thing."

Kate breathed a sigh of relief. "Yes, it is."

"There's more," he said, putting his hand on her shoulder. She stared into his eyes. "Tell me."

"Kate, I arrested Cole this afternoon."

Nineteen

"Yes, I think you'd better come in," Kate said, brushing past Peter. She switched on the lamp at the end of the sofa and waited for him to close the door. "Have a seat."

Peter sat on the love seat, and Kate eased herself onto the cushion beside him. Not wanting to brush her scraped palms against anything, she placed her hands with her palms facing up on her thighs. She felt his eyes on her.

"You're hurt." Peter picked up her hands and examined the scrapes.

"It could have been worse." Kate raised her eyes to his. "I used the Mace you gave me. If I'd reacted sooner, maybe I wouldn't have gone over the edge. I don't know what his intentions were, but the Mace may have saved my life."

Peter's face turned several shades lighter. "I called you right after Cole was booked. I knew you'd want to know. I could feel it in my bones; something was wrong when you didn't return my calls."

"I'm fine. There's nothing wrong with me that a nice long bath and a good night's sleep won't cure." She gently removed her hands from Peter's grasp. "Tell me about Cole."

"The fingerprint and DNA results came back. His fingerprints and DNA were found on Brice Denman's gun. The brass want this case closed, and Cole can't account for his whereabouts on the night of the murder. That was enough for a judge to sign an arrest warrant." Peter scooted to the edge of the seat and turned to face her, his face filled with concern. "I know he means a lot to you. The timing is terrible, but there was nothing I could do to delay anymore."

Battered and bruised from both the fall and being caught between two men she cared about, Kate's eyes welled with tears. With eyes closed, she lowered her head. "Peter, I'm tired and sore. I—" Thoughts exploded in her head. *DNA. What DNA?* She whipped her eyes to Peter, her heart throbbing. "Cole's lawyer told him to refuse a DNA test. How do you know his DNA matches what was on the murder weapon?"

"We have our ways," Peter said, looking away from her.

Kate turned her entire body to face him, grimacing as her bruises revolted. "What ways?"

Peter didn't answer.

She saw conflict in his eyes. "Please answer me."

He hung his head. "I followed you to Bello's and waited until you finished dinner. I bagged his glass before you walked out the door."

Kate rose from the love seat and marched to the door. "You should go now."

Peter stood. "If he were any other suspect, I would have done the same, Kate. You just happened to be with him." He hesitated. "Johnny Castille will be driving by periodically through the night to make sure you're OK."

Although irritated he'd arranged the drive-bys without telling her first, Kate had to admit she was relieved. "Anything else I should know?"

"No. I thought it was the prudent thing to do after the fire and your experience this afternoon." He gently took her hands in his. "I know you're angry with me, but I'm only trying to protect you."

She could see this truth in his eyes. "I know. Thank you," she said, opening the door.

He stepped through it and then turned to face her. "Keep your cellphone with you. Call 911 if you hear anything at all. Promise me that you'll call if you need me."

"I will. Good night Peter."

He gave her the briefest of embraces before turning away and disappearing down the steps and into the darkness.

Kate was disappointed. Her thirty-minute, nearly scalding shower did little to soothe her aches or make up for tossing and turning all night. She didn't have time to be tired or sore. Despite her recurring doubts about Cole, deep down she knew he couldn't have killed anyone. Guilt washed over her. She'd avoided Cole for the last several days. What could she do? *Find Chyna Moody and discover the truth.* Maybe then life would get back to normal for all of them.

Still in her bathrobe, she grabbed her cellphone from her dresser and dialed Vivi's number as she padded to the kitchen to pour a cup of coffee. Her friend picked up after the third ring. "Good morning. How'd it go in Austin? Did mom and designer behave themselves?"

Kate tilted the coffeepot and watched the strong black liquid fill her cup. "They weren't there. Carolina and I bonded over wedding plans. She asked me if I had any kids, and I told her about Vanessa. I think she liked hearing a little about my private life. Hers is so public."

"I saw Peter's car at your place when I came home last night. What's up?"

Kate filled Vivi in about the incident in Austin and Cole's arrest. "I'm fine," she said before Vivi could say anything first. "I'm concerned about Cole. He was probably arrested about the time I was tumbling off the mural." Kate took a sip of coffee. "We need to continue our investigation. We'll pick back up where we left off—Chyna Moody. Maybe she'll have more clues. If that leads nowhere, then we'll do more brainstorming. You in?"

"Give me an hour to schedule a few appointments for work. I'll drive." Vivi paused. "Are you sure you're up to this?"

"An hour is good. I'm going to call Cole's lawyer and see if it's possible for us to see Cole on our way to Dallas. He's in a holding cell in the Fort Worth Police Department waiting for his arraignment and a bond hearing."

"Sounds good," Vivi replied. "I'll beep when I pull into your driveway."

"Evan Klein, Cole's lawyer, is already at the police department," said Kate, slowly easing into Vivi's car. "He said he'd work it out so we can see Cole."

Vivi backed the Mini Cooper down Kate's driveway. "On TV, cops often allow friends and family in to see suspects so they can eavesdrop on their conversations."

"Don't worry. I don't have any information to divulge. After the fire, I backed away from both Cole and Peter. I needed some space, you know?"

"I understand." Vivi glanced at Kate before returning her eyes to the road. "Just remember they'll be listening."

"I'll remember."

The ride to Fort Worth passed quickly. Kate was relieved to sit in relative silence as Vivi entertained her with anecdotes from her ordeal with the bridezilla, whose wedding was quickly approaching. Her tales of temper tantrums, mind changing, and threats of lawsuits made Kate's trip to the Governor's Mansion seem stress free. "I don't know how you do it," Kate said.

Vivi turned onto Belknap Street. "You'd handle it better than you think."

Two blocks later, Vivi pulled the Mini Cooper into the police station parking lot. Kate called Evan Klein, who was waiting inside the station. He would meet them in the reception area.

They entered the building and went through the security check. Kate scribbled her name on the sign-in sheet and handed it to Vivi, who did the same before passing it under the clear protective panel to the bored-looking uniformed officer behind it. The woman examined the names. "Kate Stevens. The gentleman sitting under the map of Dallas is waiting for you." She pointed across the waiting area.

Evan Klein stood and met them halfway across the room and held out his hand. "Kate? I'm Evan."

"Yes, I'm Kate." She shook his hand. "This is my friend Vivi Lawrence."

Evan brought Kate up to date. The arraignment was at three that day, but he'd arranged for Kate to briefly visit Cole before they headed to Dallas. "You won't have long—a few minutes at most."

"How's he doing?" Kate asked.

"He's OK, under the circumstances. Being under a micro-scope is wearing on him, but he's keeping his cool."

Evan Klein wasn't what Kate had expected. Instead of a cocky attorney, she found Cole's college roommate to be poised but down-to-earth. Attractive in a quirky way, he had a receding hairline and an easy smile nestled between a mustache and trimmed goatee.

"Thank you for arranging for us to see him."

His eyes drifted from Kate to Vivi and back to Kate. "They only cleared you, Kate. I'm sorry."

Vivi flashed a dazzling smile. "I don't need to see him. He's really Kate's friend. I'm only along for the ride."

The receptionist called Evan and Kate to the window, where a uniformed officer was waiting to escort them to Cole. They walked silently through the halls until they came to a solid door. The officer keyed in the combination and opened it.

Evan stood discreetly by the door while Kate crossed to the table where Cole had been seated. Now he rose to his feet and she held her hands out to him. "How are you?"

He encased her hands in his. "Evan's taking care of everything." He turned Kate's hands over and raised his eyes to hers. "What happened to you?"

"I visited an outdoor mural gallery in Austin yesterday. I took a tumble off a ledge. I'm fine."

"I'm worried about you," Cole said, frowning.

"Don't be worried." Kate slid her hands from his and tried her best to give him a convincing smile. "Vivi and I are going to spend the afternoon visiting a friend in Dallas."

He raised his eyebrows. "Anyone I know?"

"Nope." She forced a grin. "We're having a girls' afternoon out."

The door opened and the officer stepped inside. "Time's up."

Kate turned her head to the officer and then looked back at Cole. "Everything will be all right. I just know it."

Cole nodded. "Me too. I'm innocent."

Kate and Evan returned to the lobby. Vivi rose to greet them. "How'd it go?"

"I'll tell you on the way to Dallas." Kate put a hand on Evan's arm. "Thank you—for arranging the visit and for taking care of Cole."

"You're welcome. I'll call you after the arraignment and bond hearing. I doubt that the judge will set bond on a murder charge."

"One challenge at a time, Evan. One challenge at a time."

Chyna's makeup-free eyes squinted in the sun. "You look familiar."

"We were at your show last week at The Edge." Kate took a deep breath. "We tried to talk to you but were told that we couldn't."

The singer studied them, the black garland of tattooed roses rippling as she moved her head. "You're a little older than most of my fans."

Kate pulled her eyes from the roses. "We wanted to talk to you about Brice Denman."

"Yeah? What about him? He's dead."

"Yes." Vivi took a step closer. "Our friend Cole has been accused of killing him. We've been talking to people who knew Brice in hopes of uncovering some information to help clear him." Vivi smiled. "We won't take much of your time. We're only trying to get to know Brice better."

Chyna looked at them without saying a word. Her eyes drifted to her neighbor's house. "You're the two who stopped by and talked to Pat?" Her voice was a curious mixture of Southern drawl and tough punk.

Kate nodded. "Yes. She told us about your grandmother. We're sorry to hear about her fall."

A smile flickered on Chyna's face and disappeared, but her eyes seemed to soften. "Thank you." She opened the door wider. "You can come in for a few minutes."

Kate and Vivi stepped into the small, musty living room in the home Chyna Moody shared with her grandmother. The worn, plaid-covered chair and green velour sofa looked like they'd been residing under the picture window since the 1970s. A collection of family photos in cheap frames covered the top of a scarred table. Stacks of *Reader's Digests* lined the wall at the end of the room. Next to them were the hints of Chyna's presence in the house—a guitar case, a music stand, a bulky duffel bag sporting a skull and crossbones, and piles of sheet music. A host of dime-store angel figurines graced the coffee table in front of the sofa.

"Have a seat on the sofa." Chyna slouched into the chair and propped her bare feet on the coffee table. Her toenails were painted black, and her pale knees showed through the threadbare jeans.

"How well did you know Brice?" Kate remembered Dexter Young's comments about Chyna's desire for revenge.

"Not too well. He was older than me. But most musicians on the circuit know each other." She was calm, cool, and collected. "We jammed together a few times. He was looking for a band."

Vivi uncrossed her legs and stood. "May I please use your restroom?"

Chyna pointed to the hallway behind her chair. "Down the hall, first door on the left."

Kate watched Vivi saunter down the hallway. She returned her focus to Chyna. "Was Brice a good musician?"

"When he was sober, he was pretty good. I only saw him clean one time."

Chyna was eyeing her with growing suspicion, but Kate kept nudging her. "His parents said he'd been writing a lot of songs lately. Were they any good?"

"Not the ones I heard." The singer smirked. "He was washed up."

"My friend Cole is also a musician. He was with us at The Edge. He said your original song was the best." Kate looked Chyna in the eye. "It was the one about your soul dying until it was released from the person who'd taken your identity from you."

"He said that, did he? And what does he know?" Chyna was getting tense.

Re-joining Kate on the sofa, Vivi momentarily blocked her from Chyna's view. Kate had left her phone set on Peter's cellphone number. As Vivi passed, Kate stuck her hand in the side pocket of her purse, pulled out the phone, pressed *Send*, and placed it out of sight on the sofa beside her.

"I was just asking Chyna about that hauntingly beautiful song she sang at The Edge and how we thought it sounded familiar," Kate said.

Chyna's nostril flared. "Oh yeah? I don't think so, unless you've been to my other shows. That song is mine."

Kate had hit a nerve, and Chyna's reaction gave her an idea.

"Really? I was sure I'd heard it somewhere else," Kate said.

"Yeah," Vivi added. "Didn't Vanessa play it for us?" Chyna was becoming more and more agitated.

"That's right," Kate said, patting Vivi's arm. "My daughter was looking for new music and stumbled on a video of some guy singing it."

Vivi bobbed her head. "Now that you mention it, that *is* where we heard it, I'm sure of it. Wasn't Brice Denman singing it? He was really good."

Chyna jumped from the chair. "You think he was good? He was nothing but a drug addict and a thief!" She pulled out the drawer of the table holding the photos and rummaged through it. "He stole my song!"

Vivi jumped up, pulling Kate's arm. "Let's go."

"Oh no you don't!" Chyna turned around, waving a gun in her hand. "I knew Grandma had this in here somewhere. Sit down."

Kate took deep, slow breaths. *Just keep her talking.* "You killed Brice over a *song*?"

The singer paced back and forth in front of the sofa. "I didn't intend to kill him. Dexter said he was going to the club to see his old nemesis, and he was sure Brice would be there. Evidently, Brice hated your friend too. I wanted to tell him that I knew he stole my song and he'd be sorry if he didn't take it offline or at least give me credit for it."

"But you did kill him," Vivi pressed.

"I followed him out to the alley to confront him, but he was already yelling at your friend and waving the gun around. I hid behind a car and watched." Chyna's eyes grew wild. "Brice was obviously wasted. Your friend went for the gun, struggled with Brice, and was able to knock the piece out of his hand. Brice ended up on the ground. The other guy kicked the gun under the car and left." Her breathing was heavy. "I grabbed the gun, thinking I could scare him good, and he'd leave my songs alone. But he was on his feet by the time I fished the gun from underneath the car and stood up. He lunged at me, trying to get the pistol. I wasn't thinking. I just reacted. Yes, I shot him! And then I tossed the gun into the Dumpster."

Kate shook her head. "But your prints weren't found on the gun."

Chyna's hysterical laugh made Kate jump. "I decided it'd be fun to dress Goth in a jazz club. I wore gloves. I was surprised when they didn't escort me out, but they didn't."

Kate didn't dare move the arm that was hiding the phone. She couldn't risk a peek. *Had Peter been able to hear anything?*

Chyna knocked several porcelain angels off the coffee table with the sweep of one hand as she pointed the gun with the other. "You had to come here and stick your nose where it didn't belong." She was losing control. "Now I'll have to shoot you too!"

Dear God, please let Peter have heard Chyna's ranting.

Twenty

Chyna stared down at the broken angels. "See what you made me do? Grandma's angels have lost their wings." The black roses around her neck trembled, and she looked up. Her eyes were as black as the tattoo. Her laugh was almost a cackle. "They're fallen angels."

The singer seemed unstable. It was only a matter of time before she totally lost it. Kate scanned the room to find something to use as a weapon. The lamp on the end table was the closest object, but it was out of her reach. Kate's purse was resting against her leg. If she swung it by the handle, she might be able knock the gun out of Chyna's hand and buy them some time. She didn't see many other options.

What was that? Kate thought the front doorknob twisted slightly. She took a longer glimpse at the door. The knob twisted again.

She pressed her leg against Vivi's, hoping her friend would understand her signal to distract the singer, who was becoming more combative. Vivi returned the gesture. She'd understood.

"*We* made you do it?" Vivi's eyes opened wide as she raised her voice. "Do you ever take responsibility for anything?"

"What do you mean?" Chyna whirled around, glaring at Vivi. "I've been taking care of myself since my mother walked out on me when I was sixteen."

"What do I mean? I'll show you what I mean." Vivi jumped up, upended the coffee table, knocking Chyna off balance and sending the remaining angels flying. Kate grabbed Vivi's shirt and pulled her toward the fireplace and out of the way as Peter burst into the room.

Chyna screamed and Peter tackled her. She was still screaming seconds later when two police officers shouted to announce their presence, ran in with weapons drawn, and cuffed the singer.

Peter leapt to his feet and crossed the room to Kate and Vivi, who were standing by the wall amid strewn issues of *Reader's Digest.* "Are you OK?"

"Yes," was all Kate could say.

Kate allowed herself to start breathing normally as the officers read Chyna her rights and pushed her out the door.

Vivi cocked her head at Peter. "Not that I'm complaining, but how did you get here so fast? I saw Kate reach for her phone, and I thought she placed a call. It seemed like an eternity while we were at gunpoint, but it couldn't have been very long."

"I was already on my way. You'd just left the Fort Worth PD when I arrived to question Cole again. He refused to answer any questions until I listened to him recount your visit and your plans to have your 'girls' afternoon out' in Dallas." Peter smiled. "He knew exactly where you were going. Even gave me the address."

Kate put an arm around Vivi's shoulders. "Well, partner, I couldn't have done it without you."

"You have no idea." Vivi pulled her phone from her pocket. "When I went down the hall to the bathroom, I set my phone to record. I think I got the entire episode, confession and all."

Peter chuckled, his mouth curling into a lopsided grin. "The one thing I've learned about you two is to always expect the unexpected."

Cole stood on the stage at the community center where Brice Denman had taken guitar lessons when he was twelve years old. It seemed a fitting place to hold Brice's memorial service. Cole was the last of three speakers who knew the late musician before he'd found drugs.

"Brice Denman was a talented musician, a loving son, and my friend." Tears welled in his eyes as he scanned the small group of people gathered in the first few rows of the auditorium to remember Brice. "His life ended tragically and much sooner than it should have. But let's remember the man, not the addiction. The love, not the drugs. The music, not the violent way he died. Let the memory of him not cause regret, but make us more aware of the pain and suffering of others, and waken a desire to champion drug abuse awareness."

His gaze settled on Helen and Douglas Denman. "Thank you for asking me to speak today. I'm humbled. I wrote a song for Brice. Dexter Young, one of Brice's friends, is going to join me on Brice's guitar. I hope you like it."

Dexter joined Cole on the stage, took a seat on a stool, and reached for the instrument in the stand beside him. He rested his right foot on the lowest rung of the stool and put the guitar strap around his neck.

By the time Cole finished singing about the creative, vibrant, and caring Brice who'd disappeared into drug addiction years ago, there wasn't a dry eye in the room. He held the last note out, letting it fade into the air before Dexter removed the guitar strap from around his neck. Cole raised his eyes above the crowd. "Thanks for letting us borrow your guitar, my friend." Cole patted Dexter on the back as he crossed the stage. He paused to hug Brice's mother and father and strode up the aisle to where Kate and Peter were standing.

He stopped at the back of the room to shake Peter's hand. "Peter, may I have a moment with Kate in the lobby?"

Peter nodded. "Certainly. I'll wait here."

Kate and Cole stepped through the double doors and into the silent, empty lobby. Cole stopped and turned to face Kate, taking her hands in his. "I'm leaving for the airport from here. My plane leaves for New York at three o'clock. I'm taking a few days to regroup, and then the band's going to pick up the tour in Santa Fe."

"Will you come back to Fort Worth?"

He nodded. "I think so. Gus and Evan are working on the timing and the legalities. I'll let you know." He looked down momentarily. When he looked up, tears were once again brimming in his eyes. "Thank you for believing in me so much that you put yourself in danger again and again. I didn't realize you were so fearless."

"Me neither, really. At least, not until I moved to Texas." She stared into his eyes. "I *had* to find the real killer. You belong onstage, not in a jail cell."

He dropped her hands. "Kate, that means the world to me, and I'll always be grateful. You're a special woman, and you deserve a man who stays in one place for more than a few months at a time." Cole brushed the hair back from her face and caressed her cheek. "Peter's a good, honest man, and he obviously has feelings for you." He smiled. "And I think you have them for him too. When you're ready, take a chance on him. I care about you enough to tell you to put the pain of your marriage behind you and open your heart. I don't think Peter would ever hurt you."

Tears stung her eyelids and threatened to slide down her

face. "You're a fine man, Cole. Stay safe, and let me know how you're doing from time to time."

"I'll send you and Peter passes to our show when the band makes it back here." He brushed her cheek with soft kiss. "Goodbye, Kate."

"Bye, Cole." Kate stood in the lobby and watched Cole Cutchins walk through the outer doors and disappear down the concrete steps. She turned toward the auditorium door to find Peter leaning against the wall beside it, watching her.

"You OK?" His voice was laced with concern.

"Yes, I'm all right." She ran her index fingers under each eye. "I imagine my makeup doesn't look too great though."

Peter pulled a handkerchief from his suit pocket and tenderly dabbed Kate's eyes. "I wouldn't worry about it."

Twenty-One

The Texas Governor's Mansion had been impressive on Kate's first visit. It was absolutely magical on Carolina's wedding day. She'd never seen so much tulle and ribbon, so many flowers, twinkle lights, and candles in one place. The fairy-tale atmosphere had been created both inside and out, although the festivities would take place outside. The ceremony, still a few hours away, would be held at sunset in the garden. Afterward, guests would join the bride and groom in celebrating their nuptials on the lawn in a large, air-conditioned tent. Kate had been paid an embarrassingly large sum to arrive early and stay to make sure the dress remained in perfect shape until Carolina walked down the aisle. She would have done it for free just for the chance to see people's reaction to the gown, Kate's most magnificent creation yet.

Peter, who'd been given security clearance, squeezed her hand as they were led by Jamie Martin into the parlor to meet with the official wedding planner, Sylvia Redmon, a high-energy brunette with every hair in place. Jamie introduced Kate and Peter to Sylvia and asked them to sit on the sofa.

Sylvia ran down the duties, informing everyone in the room of their assignment area.

"Mrs. Stevens, Jamie will escort you to the bride's room now. Officer Matthews, if you'll stay here for the time being, we'll get back with you."

As she was led out of the room, Kate smiled back at Peter. As they passed a door that was slightly ajar while walking down the hall to the bride's room, a chill ran through Kate. She felt eyes upon her. A security camera slowly tilted back and forth at the end of the hall. It was creepy being under such close scrutiny.

The bride's room was filled with flowers, food, and giggling young women not yet changed into their formal wedding attire. Carolina was in one corner holding court with her four junior bridesmaids. A quintet of older bridesmaids waited in a sitting area across the room, two on a love seat and two in wingback chairs. Carolina hugged the younger girls and crossed the room to Kate.

"I was waiting for you to get here before I unveiled the dress." Carolina was radiant, her hair and makeup perfect. The wedding dress hung in an opaque bag on a clothes rack. "Everyone is dying to see it."

"Happy wedding day." Kate smiled. "Don't you think they should get their first glimpse of it on you?"

"Yes. I just haven't had the heart to tell them. They're excited." Carolina scanned the room. "We have another room next door that's open to bridesmaids. We brought in floor-length mirrors. Their dresses are in there."

Sophia Jackson entered the room with Sylvia and the pair crossed the floor to Carolina and Kate. "Don't you think you should be getting dressed?" Mrs. Jackson looked at her daughter.

"I'll shoo the bridesmaids next door," said Sylvia. "They can come back in when you're dressed."

When the bride and her mother were the only other people in the room, Kate unzipped the opaque bag and removed it from the gown. "Mrs. Jackson, would you like to help your daughter with the dress, or do you prefer I do it?"

"I would love to help," the first lady said. "I am so proud of you, Carolina." While Carolina removed her sundress, Kate wandered to the other side of the room to give them privacy, although it wasn't requested.

"Mrs. Stevens, I need your help," Sophia Jackson called.

"Please, call me Kate," she replied, turning around to see the bride's mother holding the dress and looking a bit perplexed. "I think the best thing is for Carolina to put on her shoes and then hold her arms up while we slide the dress over her. Then I can make adjustments."

Once they were done and Kate had straightened all of the seams, she held the train and instructed Carolina to slightly rotate to look into the mirror. The mermaid-style dress flowed over her curves and accented her slender waist. The magnolia blossom lace neckline gave the sleek design a bit of frill. The bride squealed. "This is the most perfect bridal gown ever!" She turned to the side and viewed her profile. "Don't you think, Mother?"

Tears pooled in Sophia Jackson's eyes. "You're a beautiful bride." She handed her daughter a small pouch. "I know you'd planned to wear something different, but these were your great-grandmother's. This is the perfect occasion for you to have them."

Carolina opened the pouch, tilted it, and slid a double strand of small pearls into her palm. "Oh, these are gorgeous. Put them on me."

Mrs. Jackson was right. The pearls were the perfect piece of jewelry for the dress. "I'm going to give you a moment; then I'll bring in the bridesmaids," Kate said.

In the hallway, Kate nodded to the two plain-clothes officers and tapped on the next door. A woman resembling Carolina but several years older—a sister, Kate assumed—answered the door. "The bride is ready to see you now," Kate said.

The five bridesmaids and four junior bridesmaids filed into the room, breaking into *oohs* and *aahs* when they saw Carolina. Several of them held up smartphones and took photos. Kate stepped away and watched the bride enjoy the attention showered on her by her attendants.

The door opened and Kate heard a scuffle in the hallway. "I have security clearance!" A shrill voice with a thick accent silenced the tittering young women. Marisa Sanchez, draped in an exquisite champagne-colored formal dress, sashayed into the room and pushed her way past the bridesmaids.

"I just want to congratulate the bride." The designer enveloped Carolina in a quick hug. Suddenly she pushed her away, and as she did, she reached behind the dress and tugged on the train, ripping the lace. "*This* is the dress you chose over *my* designs? This rag?" She glared at Kate. "You think this dress will make you famous? Think again, my dear. You could never take my place."

Ms. Sanchez stalked in Kate's direction. "You just can't take a hint, can you?"

"The fire?" Kate said as it all came together.

"Don't you play dumb with me!" the famous designer said.

"You almost had me killed at HOPE?" Kate was flabbergasted. "And the attack in the parking garage too?"

Carolina screamed. A second later, the security guards burst into the room and grabbed the designer by the arms and hauled her away.

Kate ran to Carolina. "Don't cry. You'll ruin your makeup. It's OK. I can fix it." She examined the torn train. "Luckily it didn't rip much."

Sylvia hurried into the room with Peter. "Is everything all right here?" he asked.

"It will be," Kate said. "I'm going to fix the gown."

Peter glanced at Kate. "You OK?"

"I'm fine. She didn't touch me. Make sure everyone in the bridal party is all right." Kate retrieved her bag and pulled out a needle and thread. "This won't take long. You don't even need to take off the dress."

Peter and Sylvia left the room, and Kate concentrated on repairing the torn lace, taking time to reassure Carolina and her mother that the wedding would not be delayed and Carolina would be beautiful walking down the aisle. By the time Kate stood up and declared the rip imperceptible, Sylvia Redmon had arrived to tell Carolina that guests were arriving.

"I'm done here. All your guests will know is that you're a beautiful bride." Kate gave Carolina a quick hug and turned to leave the room.

"Kate?" Carolina called before Kate reached the door. "You're staying for the ceremony and reception, right?"

Kate cut her eyes to a smiling Sophia Jackson, who nodded her consent. "I'd be honored to remain for all of the festivities, Carolina. Thank you."

Sitting next to Peter, Kate was surprised to find herself right behind the bride's family in the formal garden outside the mansion. The wedding march began, and Carolina started down the long aisle toward the arch where her groom waited for her. Kate heard whispered comments about the beautiful bride and her exquisite dress. This was a wedding to remember. Whether or not Paige was right about this bringing Kate more wedding gown design work, creating Carolina's magnolia, mermaid-style dress would always stand out as a turning point in her career. She'd stepped out of her comfort zone.

The bride and groom kissed and Kate wiped away a tear

as Carolina and her husband walked down the aisle past her. Someday she'd have the opportunity to design Vanessa's wedding dress. Someday.

Kate and Peter mingled with wedding guests, many of them complimenting Carolina's gown. When they discovered Kate was the designer, many asked for her card. When the bridal party joined the festivities, Governor and Mrs. Jackson pulled Kate and Peter aside.

"I apologize for putting your life in danger." Sophia Jackson took Kate's hand. "I've known Marisa for years, and she'd become a friend. I knew she was hurt because I deferred to Carolina's wishes, but I didn't dream she'd try to sabotage you."

The governor shook her hand. "You've handled yourself with the utmost professionalism and discretion. My family and I are most appreciative. Thank you."

Soon the governor and his daughter were having the traditional father-daughter dance and others were joining in. Peter took Kate's hand. "How about a turn around the dance floor?"

"You dance too?" Kate asked.

"The product of a mother who insisted I take lessons as a kid."

Kate's heart swelled. "That sounds perfect."

As they waltzed, the twinkle lights flashed designs in the darkening evening. The whole scene was like a Renoir painting. A full moon rose above the horizon, washing Peter in a soft glow. Kate looked up to find his eyes looking down at her.

Their dance stopped momentarily. Kate's heart pounded and warmth surged through her as Peter's lips met hers in a soft kiss.

Cole may have been right. Maybe she should take a chance on Peter after all.

Learn more about Annie's fiction books at

AnniesFiction.com

- Access your e-books
- Discover exciting new series
- Read sample chapters
- Watch video book trailers
- Share your feedback

We've designed the Annie's Fiction website especially for you!

Plus, manage your account online!

- Check your account status
- Make payments online
- Update your address

Visit us at AnniesFiction.com